APOCRYPHA

APOCRYPHA

Blaine C. Readler

FULL ARC PRESS

APOCRYPHA

This is a work of fiction. Names, characters, places and incidents are either the product of the author's wild imagination or are used fictitiously. Any resemblance to actual events, locales, organizations, or persons, living, dead, or one foot in the grave, although inevitable and in a weird way complimentary to the author, since it shows he is not so insulated from reality that the products of his imagination are totally alien to the average mind, is nevertheless entirely coincidental and beyond the intent of either the author or the publisher.

Visit us at: http://www.readler.com

E-mail: blaine@readler.com

ISBN: 979-8-9927018-0-7

Printed in the United States of America

To all those who question what they're told with confidence and authority to believe.

Truth is an unproductive weight hobbling naive democracies.
—*Stalin commenting in private on Mahatma Gandhi's struggle for freedom from Britain.*

Chapter 1

He watched Colin from a distance, a distance from which his wings wouldn't be heard. He thought of himself as a "he," but that was just an affectation. He was no more a he than an it.

He was lucky to have found Colin, who had taken a commercial flight to get here, whereas he had to make his own way four hundred miles as the crow flies. Or as he flies.

He had heard Colin speaking to the wife of a friend, and this troublemaker was poised to contact Rachel, which meant that his hopes and plans for derailing him were now dashed. He would have taken more drastic measures, more risks in his attempts to trip the young man, but how could he have predicted how quickly Colin would deduce that Rachel was his next move? She was a wrench in the works, and now stood in the way of saving humankind.

Making decisions on his own was not always fruitful.

Rachel sat behind the wheel of her old clunker dozing, letting the similarly aging urban neighborhood, glittering under a glass sea of rooftop solar panels, slide by outside. She jerked awake when Sandy, her best friend since high school, called out to her. Shaking her head to chase away the remnants of a dream, Rachel flicked her wrist, and her com projected Sandy's live face onto the windshield. Sandy's image blinked on and off as Rachel rubbed her eyes and her wrist com struggled to keep the image steady. "Tough day in the ER?" Sandy said.

Rachel yawned. "Pretty normal."

"A tough day, then. At least no blood."

Rachel glanced down at her blue scrubs and smiled. "I wouldn't be driving home with blood still on me, now would I?"

"You're the nurse, not me. We still on for booze and debauchery?"

"I have beer and chardonnay in the fridge, but I'm too pooped for depraved shenanigans."

"I was thinking along the lines of a couple of bawdy jokes that Blake has been telling anybody he can get to listen."

The image swung to Blake behind the wheel, who looked up from his absorbed study of his tablet. "Huh? Hey, hi, Raych," he said, then, glancing at Sandy, he shrugged and went back to his reading.

"Uh, Raych . . ." Sandy began.

"Yeah?"

"Blake's college roommate is in town."

"Okay," Rachel said, shrugging. "He's coming along?"

"Raych, Colin, um, wants to meet you."

Rachel frowned. "Hey! We've been through this. No blind dates! It didn't work when we were in high school, and besides, I'm not ready for—"

"Raych, it's not a blind date," Sandy said, glancing off over her shoulder. "Colin just . . . wants to meet you."

"He's right there, isn't he."

Sandy nodded.

"Sorry, Colin!" Rachel said. "No offense."

Sandy flicked her wrist, and the displayed view swung to show Colin in the backseat, a young man with wild, curly black hair and alert eyes that seemed to flash with some hidden insight at every question, as though those very words were the next piece of a puzzle only he perceived. Coming up from some meditative place, he blinked and offered a distracted little salute.

"Um, okay," Rachel said. "Uh, it's not a date, so . . .?"

"He wants to talk about your grandfather," Blake said as the view swung back to him, still reading his tablet.

Sandy's hand swiped into view, smacking his shoulder and sending him sideways. "He is not!" Sandy said. "Colin, you promised! No talk about Justin. Understand?"

The view swung to Colin, who sighed and looked out the side window.

"Raych," Sandy said, "I'm so sorry. I thought I'd made this clear to these two clowns. Listen, maybe you'd rather we don't come?"

Rachel's heart was pounding. That's exactly what she now wanted, but she shook her head. "No, it's fine." She forced a smile. "Time to relax and let the alcohol genie out of the bottle."

Sandy watched her a moment, concerned, and then nodded and signed off.

Rachel closed her eyes and took a deep breath. Was there no escape from the transgressions of ancestors? Punishment visited upon the children and the children's children?

When she opened her eyes, the car was parking in front of her house. Pausing a moment to collect herself, she got out and saw the beat-up old trike motorcycle with

3

a cart full of boxes and tools hitched at the back. "Jubal!" she called. "I'm home."

A burly middle-aged man dressed in dirty work clothes and wiping his hands on a grimy rag emerged from a cellar door along the side of the house. "Hey there, Rachel," he said. "Just finished."

"Apparently the house hasn't blown up."

He cocked an eyebrow. "I should report this, you know."

She couldn't tell if he was serious. "Really?"

He grinned. "Nah. Sulfide batteries can't blow up. They're classic. Antiques, really. Your house could be a museum." He frowned. "Could've burned the house down, though. Once one gets goin', it's a wild drunken battery party. They go down like dominoes. It might *seem* like they've blown up."

She nodded slowly, sighing.

"You okay?" he said.

She nodded again. "Just tired, Jubal. Thanks for asking."

He watched her a moment. "Sure you're okay, Rachel? I mean, you know, all alone in the house."

She smiled at his concern. "Yes, I'm fine. Good riddance."

Jubal shook his head at the injustice. "That was no reason for him to leave."

She lifted her shoulders, accepting her fate. "A prion ancestor is reason enough."

"But he was never confirmed, right?"

"You know how it goes. When your grandfather is even just accused – it taints the whole clan."

'What happened to for 'better or for worse'?"

She lifted her shoulders again. "He claimed that it was affecting his clients."

What more was there to say? She should have told Mark at the beginning. He might not have married her. And that's why, of course, she hadn't told him. It was stupid to believe that he wouldn't have found out eventually. It happened so quickly, though, as though someone was waiting for her to finally feel secure and happy.

Jubal studied her a moment and shook his head, not convinced. "Hey," he said, breaking the sour mood, "how much they asking for that little gem?"

He was pointing to a small, aging house down the street. "Three million, I think. Are you interested?"

He chuckled. "Interested, sure. Able? Not in this lifetime."

Rachel had known Jubal for years. He'd been their handyman back before her mom died and left her alone in the house. She bit her lip, considering. "Maybe I can help with the downpayment. We have to get you out of the tract."

"Don't I wish. I appreciate it, Raych, but even if I could get a mortgage, the payments would be at least twice what I could afford." He eyed her and gestured towards her battered car. "Besides, it's not like you're swimming in riches."

She nodded, resigned, then brightened. "Hey, did your daughter – Annie? – get the scholarship?"

"Angie. We don't know yet. She's sharp. With luck, we'll get her out. Get her an education and a good job, then I can venture out of the tract now and then to visit."

"Good plan. I doubt she'll leave you behind in the trenches, though."

He smiled. "Maybe. We can only hope."

Inside, Rachel tossed her bag onto a chair in the living room and flopped down on the sofa. The eight-foot screen on the wall came to life with a mosaic of entertainment and news feeds, which plipped away as Rachel flipped her thumb this way and that to select and reject them each in turn, eventually leaving just one news/talk show, which, with a final flick, filled the screen. Three attractive people sat "debating," but really sharing mild outrage at a city council plan to maintain the existing boundaries of the Clawson Tract. The show switched to an ariel shot, showing a decrepit slum, the very tract where Jubal lived. The show switched back, where councilman Breyer argued for enlarging the tract. The intent of the whole "debate" was clearly in support of Breyer's plan for expansion.

"Make room for more people to huddle in desperate poverty," Rachel muttered, and flicked her thumb to kill the show.

The screen was now dark except for a tiny face waiting patiently in a far corner. Rachel smiled, and flicked her thumb up, launching the image life-size, a homely woman exuding easy friendliness.

"Hey, Tiff!" Rachel said. "A sight for sore eyes."

"That goes both ways," Tiffany replied. "Looks like you had a rough day."

Rachel smiled and gestured dramatically down the front of her scrubs shirt. "No blood. Can't have been too bad."

"I'll make a wild guess that blood isn't the most stressful part of your job. Any wailers today?"

Rachel grinned. "You know me too well, Tiff."

"We've been friends a long time."

"We did have one." Her grin dissolved, remembering. Wailers was the label they'd given to relatives destroyed by sudden, overwhelming grief. "Parents of a toddler who drowned. They found her face-down in a little pool that formed when a ditch overflowed. No more than three or four inches deep. They'd tried to resuscitate her, and had broken most of the little girl's ribs. At this point, it had been like a half hour after they'd found her, but they couldn't accept that she was dead. They pleaded and begged for us to save her. I tell you, it just tears your heart out."

Tiffany watched Rachel a moment, her calm strength reaching through the screen with sympathy. "You're an angel, you know, Raych. What would we be without people like you willing to put their psyches on the line every day to help us?"

Tiffany watched her a moment. "Mark really has you down, doesn't he."

Rachel bounced her shoulders. "I don't blame him. Not really. But yeah, it's hard."

"You're right not to blame him I guess. A prion grandfather is, well, kind of scary."

"It was never confirmed."

"Of course, but what if he was? You know . . ."

"Tiff! For God's sake, you don't think I'm corrupted! I'm twenty-nine years old. It would have shown years ago—"

"No, of course not. I know you, Raych, maybe as much as you know yourself. I'm just saying that from other people's perspective, well, I would expect them to be cautious. There's a reason why they call them prions, after all. You, a nurse, obviously know this."

She was all too aware. Prions were behind mad cows disease and Creutzfeldt–Jakob disease. They were insidious, nature's dark and evil side—misshapen proteins that transferred their mis-folds to other proteins, and they then went on to infect yet others, a truly horrifying molecular zombie. To compare this monstrosity to her grandfather was beyond comprehension.

"He used to bounce me on his knee," she said. "He would sing a little song about an itsy bitsy spider."

"Your grandfather, Justin Hoch?"

"Yes. He was the most gentle person I've ever met."

"He wouldn't have disseminated to you, a child."

Rachel frowned. "You're implying that he really was a . . . a— "

"Prion? No, of course not. In any case, it's not like it's a transmitted biological condition. It's a disease all right, but a disease of a society, instigated by the dangerous ideas of a few mentally warped individuals . . . but here I am lecturing a nurse. Sorry. It's just, you know, all so scary."

Just then the screen announced visitors at the door, displaying a live feed of her three guests.

"Oops, I have to go," Rachel said.

"Sandy, right? And Blake. And . . .?"

"Colin. Blake's college roommate. He seems to be . . . well, self-absorbed."

"He looks interesting, Raych. You should give him some slack."

"Tiff! I'm not in the market for—"

"I mean he seems intelligent."

"It's just drinks and conversation. We're not debating global trade."

Tiffany gave a little knowing nod. "Of course. Talk to you later, Raych."

When Rachel let them in, Colin paused just inside the door, peering around, as though expecting something different. "Something wrong?" Sandy asked with a tinge of annoyance.

Colin looked at her, seeming surprised at her question. "No. Not at all."

Rachel held out her hand. "Hey, Colin. I'm Rachel."

He looked at her a moment, then gave a little nod and shook her hand without replying. As Colin and Blake headed off to the living room, Rachel whispered to Sandy, "You didn't tell me he was so fetching."

Sandy looked at Rachel with one raised eyebrow. "You said no blind dates. Besides, I don't know, I don't trust him somehow."

"I have a four-year hole in my life," Blake said. They were sitting in the living room drinking wine. Rachel struggled to keep from staring at her new guest. "Colin disconnected our screen. I essentially dropped out of society the whole time I was in college. The IT people would come around and hook it up, and he'd disconnect it as soon as they left."

Sandy's eyes narrowed. "Why?"

Colin didn't seem to hear. He was staring off at the walls and furnishings.

"Words, Colin," Blake said, as though this was a common reminder.

Colin turned slowly to them. "You know why, Blake."

"Right," Blake said in an exaggerated imitation of Colin's voice, "we're here to study, not be entertained."

"And this is some kind of aberration?" Colin said. He turned to Rachel. "Your grandfather, I know you'd rather not talk about him, but—"

"And you don't have to," Sandy said. "Colin, you promised."

"Actually, I never did," he said.

Rachel shrugged. "It's all right. We're all friends."

"He doesn't believe in squads," Sandy said turning to him, a challenge.

"Really?" Rachel said, curious.

"Small minds," he said, "intoxicated with power. Nothing but neighborhood bullies."

Rachel suppressed a grin, not wanting to piss off Sandy, but this was exactly what she thought. She had never been so bold to speak the words, not with the suspicions left hanging after her grandfather's death. That dark legacy sustained a persistent low level of anxiety, a jolt of alarm any time the local squad was mentioned.

"And who's going to prevent another Dark Tide, then?" Sandy said.

Colin spread his arms wide. "Who's going to *create* another Dark Tide?"

They all glanced at Rachel, and for the first time Colin's aloof confidence seemed to faulter. Rallying, he said, "It turns neighbors against each other. We're no better than Stalinist Russia."

"What kind of Russia?" Rachel said.

"Something from the last century," Sandy said. "He studies history," she added like it was a slur.

That seemed to rattle him. "Without history, we are doomed to repeat all the mistakes down through the ages."

Sandy glared at him with wild eyes. "Obsession with the past will eventually pull you into the madness of the Dark Tide."

"No," he said quietly, "understanding what happened thirty years ago is the only way to prevent it from happening again." He shook his head in disgust. "Don't be a fool."

Rachel thought that Sandy was going to explode. She sat utterly still, eyes practically popping from their sockets.

"Now it's too many words, Colin," Blake said. He stood up. "Maybe it's time to wrap it up for the evening."

"Exactly," Sandy growled. "Before somebody crosses a line."

Colin pretended horrified alarm. "And reveals themselves as a . . . a . . . *prion*? Oh my!"

Sandy jumped to her feet and leaned over him, jabbing a finger inches from his face. "Joke about it, asshole. Have your fun until they drag you away."

He looked past her quivering finger as though it didn't exist. "By your selfless patriotic neighbors."

"Okay," Blake announced, "that's it. We're going."

Sandy shook her fist at Colin as Blake pulled her toward the door.

Colin stood up and turned to Rachel. "I . . ." He glanced at the retreating couple, shrugged, and trotted off after them.

Rachel sat thinking about what had just happened as the sound of the car outside whirred away. The silence was broken by a light ding, a reminder. Tiffany's face floated in a little window in the corner of the screen. Rachel flicked her thumb and her friend expanded life-sized. "I didn't mean to intrude," Tiffany said, "but you left the link open and, well, I confess, I couldn't resist tuning in."

Rachel waved it off. "Tiff, you're welcome anytime. You're my best friend."

"Not Sandy?"

"Not sure. She really went ballistic. Did you catch that?"

"Afraid I did. Raych, I'm impressed that you kept your cool."

"I was just watching."

"No, I mean about what Colin was saying."

"I don't know. He seemed to be making some sense."

"Really?"

"I mean, how can we avoid another Dark Tide if we don't understand what caused the first one."

"I thought we did understand—social psychosis."

"Sure—mass anxiety hysteria, like we learned in school."

"Exactly. And we know what fed it, right?"

"Of course, Tiff. We all know—fake news."

"You bet. The fake news cancer germs spread faster than anybody could stop them."

"Tiff, there's no such thing as cancer germs."

"You know what I mean."

"Yeah. You're right, Tiff. I got carried away.

"I can understand why, Raych. Colin, he's very persuasive."

Rachel grinned. "And cute."

Tiffany looked concerned. "Raych, be careful. He might be sort of dangerous as well."

She nodded. "Yeah, you're right again. In any case, the way the evening ended there, I don't think I'll be seeing him again."

As Tiffany signed off and the screen went dark, Rachel thought that it was a shame. The guy really was engaging. And cute.

Blaine C. Readler

Chapter 2

He watched as Rachel left for the hospital the next morning. Colin was a troublemaker all right. The young man hadn't directly created the pending tsunami, but when you poke a hornet nest, somebody gets stung. Things were going to hell in a handbasket fast. He'd have to wait a bit, though, see where the hornets landed.

When Rachel arrived at the nurses station, Johnathan, the orderly, took one look at her, and walked quickly away. She didn't think much of it, as he could be grumpy until his third cup of coffee, and it was best to leave him be anyway.

She knew something was up, though, when Beatrice, the supervisor, called her name from down the hall. The tone was both angry and bursting with authority, a tone she used only when somebody was in deep shit, apparently this time her.

Rachel turned to find a middle-aged man following along close behind Beatrice. When they got to her, Beatrice paused, and glanced around making sure nobody was listening. Still angry, but containing herself, she leaned in and said quietly, "Go on home."

Rachel stared at her. "Why? My shift starts in—"

"Just . . ." She glanced at the man, who nodded. "Just go home."

"But, I don't know why—"

"You have three minutes to be out the door," the man said.

Rachel looked at him, a large, heavy man with a military style crewcut. "Or what?" She said. To Beatrice, "Who's he?"

"Now two minutes and fifty-five seconds," the man said.

Beatrice raised one eyebrow, a gesture that said she was treading on thin ice.

"But I . . ." she started, but gave up, turned, and walked away.

In a daze, Rachel made her way back to her car. Everybody turned away as she passed, desperately avoiding any hint of association.

Sitting in the driver's seat, she realized that the car had been asking ever more insistently where she wanted to go. "Home," she finally whispered.

Her brain seemed frozen in a relentless spin. She couldn't have been more shocked than if she'd woken to find her legs missing. What happened? What had she done to receive that kind of response? Had she murdered someone while cloaked in a state of amnesia? Of course not. She could remember every hour of the last few days. Besides, the police would have hauled her away.

There was only one possible explanation, and she resisted facing it. But after fabricating ever more unlikely scenarios, she couldn't hide forever.

They thought she was a prion.

Having accepted this, she felt weak and nauseous. But why? *Why?* She couldn't think of anything she'd done that might in any way be construed as prion behavior.

Suddenly her wrist beeped and Sandy's angry face appeared. "What the hell did you do last night after we left?"

"Nothing!" Rachel said, barely able to speak. "I went to bed!"

"Rachel, friends don't lie to friends. I've been getting pings all morning. We can't take this anymore. We've hung in there over the years as people asked loaded questions about you and your grandfather. But Blake's job depends on the goodwill of his clients. We can't afford to be associated with . . ."

It hung in the air, just needing a nudge to become real. "A prion," Rachel said, choking on the word.

Her friend just stared at her, letting silence serve as judge and jury.

"I didn't do anything!" Rachel cried. "I have no idea what's going on. Sandy, you have to help me."

In answer, Sandy flicked her thumb. Her face was replaced by a video of Rachel talking to someone off-screen:

"—no, let's see . . . wait, I've got it! We can create some footage showing councilman Breyer accepting kickbacks to approve the sewer upgrade. Don't you see?"

From off screen, someone says, "What about the local squad?"

"Those bumbling neighborhood bullies? With Breyer out of the running, our guy will be a shoe-in—"

The display changed to the same news/talk program that Rachel had watched when she came home the day before. The discussion now was about how Councilman Breyer was being undercut by lies being propagated by a small cadre of individuals. The lead presenter nodded off-screen, and the audience was shown a snippet of the fabricated video of Rachel talking about fake kickbacks. The presenters wondered if the Oakland squad was on this, hinting that they may have a prion in their midst.

When Sandy returned to the display, Rachel was sputtering with outrage. "That's not me!"

Sandy had calmed after delivering the damning proof. "That's what they all say, Raych." She flicked her thumb, and her face disappeared.

Rachel's face was still buried in her hands when the car announced that they had arrived home. Her brain felt like a lump of cheese tossed into a blender.

∞

Rachel sat on the sofa, still dazed. The wall screen was filled with the myriad tiled shows that always came on when she entered the house. Wearily, she made a chopping motion with one hand and the screen went dark. A moment later, though, Tiffany appeared in a small square in the corner. Rachel flicked to expand her friend.

"Hey, girl! Why the glum face?" Tiffany said.

"You haven't heard? Check the news here in Oakland."

Her friend glanced off and flicked a few times. Her face turned serious as the sounds of the kickback video clip came through. She turned back to Rachel. "I don't understand."

"I don't either! It's all made up. I swear!"

Tiffany considered this. "There must be some mistake."

"Somebody created that video and . . . put me on it."

Tiffany shook her head. "I don't think that's possible."

Rachel thought her head might burst. "Really?"

Tiffany gave her a you-know-better look. "Really, Raych. This is my field, after all."

"Well, maybe it's a Dark Tides sort of thing?"

Her friend turned stern. "Raych, don't talk like that. Not with . . . this." She seemed to deliberate. "You know, there's implications that you could be a prion."

Rachel felt herself go hard and cold. "Tiff, you don't believe me, do you."

Tiffany's face softened and she smiled. "Raych, I do believe you. I know you. We're best buds. I trust you completely."

Rachel stared at Tiffany's smiling face and sighed. "Thanks Tiff. I don't know what I'd do without you. You may be the only friend I have left."

"You're being overly dramatic. I'm sure—"

She was interrupted by the doorbell. Wearily, Rachel got up and when she opened the front door, Colin was standing there. "You," she said, unable to hide her irritation. After glancing up and down the street, she motioned for him to enter. "What the hell have you done?"

Stone-faced, Colin walked in. "Apparently I made the mistake of talking to you."

"What's that supposed to mean?"

"It means I didn't do anything except talk to you."

"I don't understand."

"I'm not sure I do either."

When he walked into the living room Tiffany said, "You must be Colin."

He nodded and glanced questioningly at Rachel.

"Raych," Tiffany said, "I'll talk to you later. I'll leave you two alone. It's nice to have a man around again." The screen want dark.

Colin turned to Rachel, one eyebrow raised.

"Never mind," she said. "So, I suppose it's only a coincidence that just as you arrive in town, somebody is—somehow—making fake videos to make me look like a criminal?"

"No, I don't think it's a coincidence. It's just that I don't know why."

"You don't know why—then why are you here?"

"Your grandfather. Look, let's sit down. I'll try to explain what I do know."

Sitting on the sofa, he said, "Your grandfather is a piece to a puzzle I've been working on for months, maybe the last piece."

"He's been dead twenty years, but his infamy seems immortal."

Colin ignored this. "Did he ever talk about his colleagues? Specifically a man named Francis Tichells?"

Rachel shook her head, and he thought a moment. "I'm working on my doctoral thesis, or I was before my advisor professor at Rutgers withdrew—"

"You want to be a historian. You want to mangle the past."

She didn't really mean to say that. It was the sort of catchphrase she heard so often that it seemed to form in her mouth of its own accord.

Colin's brow furrowed. "Why can't people see that we're the ones looking for truth. If they'd take just a little time to understand what we do—what?"

She was shaking her head. "It's okay. I don't swallow everything that's fed to us like Sandy does."

He seemed to relax. She realized that he had been stiff and wary. "That's a huge relief," he said.

"Why?"

"You've been targeted falsely. Just as I was when I chose the Dark Tide for my thesis."

"The Dark Tide? Boy, you're either brave or insane."

"I'm not insane, but in retrospect stupid might be a third choice. At first my advisor grudgingly agreed, but it didn't take long before rumors stalked the university halls, and he withdrew before losing his own position."

"But you continued. The stupid part."

"I was hooked. This was a historian's dream, a completely untapped period—"

"Untapped for the very sane reason that even talking about it risks becoming a pariah."

"The Medusa effect."

"Right. What was so intriguing that you'd risk your career? Of course, don't tell anybody I asked."

Colin hesitated.

"I was joking," Rachel said. "What was so intriguing?"

"The accepted view is that the twenties and thirties were so vile, so immersed in the deepest deceit and lies, that even reading about it puts you at risk of becoming defiled yourself, a prion. A modern-day fear of the devil."

"That wasn't the case? I always figured that it was exaggerated, but that it was basically true."

"Oh, the deceit and lies for sure. Politically, culturally, religiously – people were split into camps immersed in their own fantasy worlds. It was like nobody cared about objective truth anymore."

"So the common view is indeed correct, then."

"It's not that simple. Nobody seems to question how simply learning about human behavior could somehow be infectious. In fact, it's exactly the opposite. That's how we learn from our mistakes."

"What history is supposed to be about."

Again Colin hesitated.

"I wasn't being sarcastic," she said. "The Holocaust was real."

"Right. What mystified me was how the Dark Tide period subject became taboo in the first place. And, the intensity! Like just bringing up the subject will turn you into some lie-spewing anarchist."

"It doesn't?" Rachel said with faux innocence.

He ignored her. "But, finally, crucially, it was the social hammer coming down instantly, almost before my thesis subject was even announced, as though somebody was watching and waiting to jump in and spread the word."

"You never found the source? Who started the storm?"

"The damndest thing – as though the message went out everywhere simultaneously."

Colin sat staring, as though reliving that time.

Tentatively, Rachel said, "Apparently you didn't give up. You're here."

"Right. The stupid part. I almost did give up, actually. The hurdles were exasperating, wearing me down. But then I found the gold."

"A pot-full, or a calf when you came down off the mountain?"

"Rat turds."

"Excuse me?"

"Far in the back of a little basement room used for storing air conditioning ducting was a box covered with rat droppings – thick enough to deter anybody who might be the least curious."

"Inside were golden rats."

"Something better – books from the Dark Tide. Technical references, actually. Not something that usually catches the eye of a historian, but one book covered a subject new to me. Are you familiar with the term, 'artificial intelligence'?"

Rachel shook her head.

"Here was a whole field of engineering that I'd never even heard of," Colin said. "Not only that, but the context implied that this was an ongoing development, not some theoretical pie-in-the-sky mental game, like—I don't know—quantum spaceship drives or something."

"Interesting, but where do you go with something like that?"

Colin eyed her a moment. "What any historian would do, I tried to track down the two authors."

"They'd be, like, seventy years old."

"At least. One, Francis Tichells, has been missing a long time and presumed dead. The other one you've met, Rachel."

"I have?"

"Rachel, it's your grandfather, Justin Hoch."

She stared at him, then blinked. "You sure?"

He held out his palms. "Maybe you can tell *me*. What was his profession?"

"He was a teacher, a professor at Oakland University."

"What field?"

She blinked again. "I . . . um, something about math—look, by the time I was old enough to ask, he and everything about him was, you know, taboo."

Colin nodded. "That must be him. Somebody went to a lot of effort to quash this subject, this 'artificial intelligence.'"

"Why?"

"That's the question. Why? So much changed during that period, it might be that this was a subject that just got caught up in the backlash to the madness. It might not mean anything."

"But you're here. You don't think so."

"Was it a coincidence that your grandfather was labeled a prion and his field of expertise disappeared?"

"Could be."

"Do you really believe that?"

She sighed. "I'm not sure what to believe. I've had all of about two minutes to think about it."

"I understand."

He studied her.

"What?" Rachel said.

He gestured towards the blank screen on the wall. "Take a look at your criminal evidence."

Rachel's heart skipped. "No."

"Why?"

"It's not me!"

"It looks like you."

"Yes, but . . ."

"Take a look."

She glared at him, fuming, then flicked her thumb and said, "News, Breyer, kickback."

Instantly multiple feeds appeared, with the captured video playing occasionally.

"It looks a lot like you, doesn't it?" Colin said.

She just watched, feeling the blood pounding in her neck.

"In the book, your grandfather explained how artificial intelligence could synthesize images."

She looked at him. "You think somebody used this artificial intelligence to create a video of me, out of thin air?"

He raised his eyebrows suggestively.

She thought a moment, and then shook her head. "I have a good friend who says that's impossible."

"He has qualifications to know?"

"He's a she, and yes, she's an engineer – works with software that cleans up photos and videos." Without waiting for agreement, she called, "Tiff! You there?"

"There's lots of different fields," Colin said. "Just because your friend's an engineer—"

Tiffany appeared full size. "Hey, Raych—hello Colin. What's up?"

"I need your engineering expertise. You said earlier that you didn't think that it would be possible to create that fake video of me from scratch."

"That's right. Why?"

Rachel glanced at Colin. "Have you ever heard of 'artificial intelligence'?"

"*Artificial* intelligence? Sounds like some people I know, but otherwise, no."

"Of course she wouldn't have heard of it—" Colin began, but Rachel held up her hand.

"You're sure that it's just not possible?" she said.

Tiffany shrugged. "It's dangerous to claim anything is impossible. It comes down to probability. Think about what it would take." She flicked her wrist, and the fake video played next to her. "Frame by frame that video would need to created pixel-by-pixel. Well, sure, it *could* be done, but think about the amount of time—days and days of arduous effort."

Rachel jerked as Colin grabbed her arm. "What!" she cried. His grip hurt.

He stared at her, then turned to Tiff. "Sorry, but . . . I just remembered that I have something that I need to show Rachel. It's . . . important. Outside."

"What are you talking about?" Rachel barked, jerking her arm from his grasp.

His look was a plea.

She sighed. "Sorry, Tiff," she said. "I'll be right back after I see what this maniac wants."

Outside, Colin closed the door behind them and turned to Rachel. "They've been listening," he said quietly, glancing back at the house.

"What *are* you talking about? Who's been listening?"

"I don't know. Somebody. Through your screen."

She peered at him. "Are you taking drugs?"

"What? No! Of course not. In the fake video, what do you say . . . what do they *have* you saying?"

She shook her head, annoyed. "I don't know, something about me supposedly creating some footage of Breyer taking kickbacks—"

"Hold it. They have you describing the local squad, and you call them 'bumbling neighborhood bullies.'"

She thought about it and shrugged. "So?"

"Don't you see? That's exactly what I called them in your living room earlier, minus the bumbling part."

He was right.

"When have you ever called a squad neighborhood bullies?" he said. "When have you ever even thought of that?"

She blinked. "That means . . ."

"Exactly. Do you think your friends Sandy and Blake made the fake video?"

She took a step back, eyes wide. "No! Of course not! That's ridiculous."

"Of course it is. I never thought they did. If not them, then who else knew those words were spoken?"

She took a deep breath and let it out slowly. "I don't have a clue."

"Neither do I, but it had to be somebody listening through your screen."

"It was off!"

"I don't think it's ever off unless you unplug it. How did you call Tiffany just now? You simply spoke to the blank screen. It was obviously listening."

"Sure, but that's the screen that listens. You're saying that somebody was somehow listening *through* the screen?"

"People hear you when you're talking with them— with Tiffany just now, for example."

It seemed utterly crazy, someone listening all the time, even when the screen was off. But maybe it made sense. How else to explain "neighborhood bullies"?

Colin was chewing his lip, and seemed to make up his mind. "Come on," he said, and went back inside. In the living room, he told Tiffany, "Sorry, but we have to deal with something here. Rachel will get back to you later."

"Raych," Tiffany said, "what's happening? Is there trouble—?"

Colin had yanked out the power cord, and the screen went dead.

"That was pretty rude," Rachel said.

"Yeah it was. I wish we could afford to worry about niceties."

He picked up his bag, reached inside, and pulled out a beat-up old composition notebook.

"What's that?" Rachel asked.

He was holding the notebook as though it was all the answer she needed. "It's yours," he finally said, handing it to her.

"Mine? I never had a notebook like this—"

"It was your grandfather's."

She stared at the cover, where his name was written at the top. "Where did you get it?"

"That's another story. Nobody would talk to me when I began searching out the authors of the AI—the artificial intelligence—reference book. I was facing slammed doors at any mention of that time. That is until I found Francis Tichells' daughter, Ashley."

"She was willing to talk?"

"She's dying of pancreatic cancer. She didn't give a damn what people might think. Her father, Francis, abandoned her and her mother when she was nine. He just disappeared, not coincidentally soon after your grandfather died. He didn't disappear completely. For a few years, he'd send money, but then that tapered off, and finally stopped altogether. He'd taken his books and notebooks, but had missed this one, fallen behind a dresser. Justin may have given it to him, knowing that they were about to come after him."

"My grandfather committed suicide."

"Tichells didn't think so."

"He thought that my grandfather was . . . murdered?"

Colin shrugged. "He thought so, and figured he was next."

Rachel stared at the notebook in her hands, and then opened it, leafing through, finding diagrams, equations, and jargon that she could only guess at. "Who was coming after my grandfather?"

Taking a deep breath, Colin said, "That's the million-dollar question. Francis Tichells believed it had something to do with their research."

"Artificial intelligence."

"Right."

Colin watched her a moment, seeming to consider. "There was one more thing that Ashely told me. Tichells and Justin had been working with the FBI."

Rachel shook her head. "No way. I would have known about that."

"She was pretty confident. They were doing it on the side, keeping it on the lowdown. Your mother never said anything?"

"Ha. After grandpa died, she refused to talk about him. I think she was angry – furious – that he checked out and left us on our own."

"Your father . . .?"

"Left us about that time. Same reason as my own ex-husband – couldn't handle the stigma."

"But your mother blamed your grandfather, not her husband?"

"She understood his motives for leaving." Rachel smiled, a sardonic grin. "Just like I understand my own spouse . . . but I'll have to give that a second consideration."

Just then Colin's wrist dinged. He flipped up his thumb, and a man's face appeared, displayed on the back of the sofa. "Hey, James," Colin said, "what's up?"

"I think I found another reference for you." He looked off to the side. "How about 'stochastic contour dependencies for texture modeling'? Whatever that means."

"Yeah," Colin said. "Sounds about in line, thanks. Hey, I'm with someone. Can I get back to you?"

"Sure. Uh, Colin . . .?"

"Yeah?"

"Hey, you ok, my friend? I mean, I don't know, this stuff seems . . . risky, maybe?"

Colin nodded. "Thanks for the concern, James, but no need to worry. Everything's fine."

After James's face disappeared, Colin said, "That's a friend. Lives in Florida."

"Everything's fine?" Rachel said.

"The less I get others involved, the less they're at risk. But no, if everything were fine, I wouldn't be here."

"Apparently I'm not one of the lucky ones who you keep uninvolved."

He frowned in concern. "Yeah, I'm really sorry about that—"

"I was joking. I want to find out the truths about my grandfather."

Colin nodded, thought a moment, then took the notebook, leafed through, and handed it back, pointing. "What do you make of that?"

She read and looked up. "Who are the 'Hoovers'? He doesn't have a very high opinion of them."

He was grinning. "Hoover? J—"

"Edgar! Of course, he's talking about the FBI."

"Would seem so." He took the notebook, flipped a few pages and handed it back.

"What's the 'axe'?" she said after reading part of the page.

"I don't know, but he describes sending versions to it, obviously software. They – he and Tichells – were developing some kind of software program."

He took the book and flipped to nearly the end before handing it back. She read one page, and then another. "They finished the first phase," she said. "Who is Cixi?" Putting her finger on the page, she read, "'Cixi would need to be in an uncoordinated, segmented state to be effective.'"

"Another mystery. He refers to her at different places."

"She's a 'she'? A mistress?"

Colin smiled. "I don't think so. I imagine that a mistress that needed to be in an uncoordinated, segmented state wouldn't be a mistress very long. I think it's sort of a code word, like 'Hoover.'"

Rachel thought a moment. "That name – it's somehow familiar." She flicked her wrist, thumb and little finger extended and directed, "History—a woman named Cixi."

Her wrist said, "Cixi is a county-level city in the Zhejiang province of China—"

"Stop. I said a woman named Cixi."

"There is no woman named Cixi in history," her wrist said with confidence.

Rachel shrugged.

"I already tried that," Colin said. He reached out and tapped the book. "I think we need to find this axe. It's the only thing we have to go on."

"You think it was my grandfather's?"

"It's his notebook. He refers to it as 'my axe.'"

She shook her head. "My grandfather was an academic, not a chopping-wood kind of guy."

Colin considered, nodding slowly. "It needn't have been an actual axe— how would he store software code? No, it's obviously another code word."

Rachel shrugged.

"Did your grandfather have an office, here in the house?"

"Upstairs. But my mom took it over after he . . . died."

"Can we take a look?" Colin said, heading for the stairs without waiting for an answer.

Rachel followed him up and into what was essentially a roomy attic, with dormer windows, hardwood floor, and floor-to-ceiling bookshelves. "This was your grandfather's," he said, pointing to a large desk in the corner.

"Yes, but, like I said, my mom took it over. It's all her stuff."

Colin went through the drawers, scanned the shelves to each side, and even got down and peered underneath.

As he was searching, Rachel went to the ancient set of Britannica encyclopedias that lived snuggly in a shelf all its own. She pulled a volume and flipped the pages. "Huh," she said, reading.

Colin came over. "What did you find?"

"My com was wrong," she said, holding the book for him to see. "Cixi was the dowager de facto ruler of China during the eighteen hundreds, out of view behind her son, the emperor." She read some more. "She was ruthless— 'Cixi' doesn't sound like a fuzzy-friendly code name."

"Yeah," Colin said, seeming to lose interest, "our coms aren't perfect, I guess. We need to figure out what this axe might be."

He clasped his hands together and placed a forefinger on each side of his nose as he stared, thinking. Still in contemplation, he walked to an old, over-stuffed sofa and sat down, but essentially fell into it as the cushion gave way beneath him. He jumped up with a cry and lifted the cushion.

"The under structure gave way long ago," Rachel said, laughing. "It was too much trouble for my mom— and me—to get rid of."

Colin peered around the cluttered attic. "What would a metaphorical axe look like?"

"We don't even know if it's actually here."

Colin shrugged. "Where else? A safety deposit box? Buried out in the yard?"

Axe. The word swam back across the years from Rachel's childhood. "One of my earliest memories is of my grandfather playing music. It was him and another man, a friend. They played and sang together, and my mom claimed that they sounded like two wounded dogs."

"What was his friend's name?"

She thought a moment. "I remember. At first I thought it was silly to call a man itchy, but it was actually Tichy."

Colin's eyes went wide.

Rachel smacked her forehead. "Of course! That would have been Francis Tichells. But what I was remembering was what they called their guitars—"

"Axes!" Colin nearly shouted. "Of course."

Rachel turned and pointed. There above one of the bookshelves, tucked away among the clutter and dust so long that she'd forgotten about it was her grandfather's old guitar case. Colin took it down, laid it on the floor, unlatched the top, and pulled out the old Martin acoustic. He peered inside through the sound hole, and then turned it upside down and shook it. He looked at her, disappointed.

"Hold on," she said, taking it from him. On the side was a plastic panel. She pushed a little lever, and a tiny door popped open.

"The battery compartment," Colins said.

She looked at him suggestively and turned the guitar over. A flattened plastic cylinder fell out onto the floor. Colin picked it up and removed a piece of paper taped around it.

"What is it?" she asked.

Colin held it up. "It's called a flash drive."

"It drives?"

"No, it's computer memory. They fell out of use during the Dark Tide. I think there were even laws passed. When information could be weaponized, memory storage was like an ammunition cache."

She picked up the paper, unrolled it, and read.

"Fuck!" she whispered.

"What is it?" Colin asked.

"It's from my grandfather. It's to Tichy. He says that if he—Tichy—finds this it means that they've come for him—"

"So much for committing suicide."

"But listen, he says that Tichy will know what to do with this—the flashing drive, I guess."

"That's 'flash drive.'"

"Whatever. Get this—he writes 'This is our last hope.'"

"Last hope? 'Fuck' indeed."

Just then, from below they heard a pounding on the front door. Rachel ran to the dormer window. Below were half a dozen people, and among them she saw Sandy, the man that had stood by while she'd been fired, and a man wearing an FBI jacket. As she watched, a policeman stepped back from the door and picked up a long metal bar.

"It's the squad!" she said, turning around.

Colin had already jumped into action. He pulled down a multifarious mobile display made with a long, heavy rope hanging in the corner, yanked off some of the delicate paper animals, then ran to a window at the back of the house.

Just then, from below came the screeching sound of the front door being pried open.

Blaine C. Readler

Chapter 3

He watched and listened to the disparate faces of law enforcement, both sanctioned and self-appointed, debating at Rachel's front door. The squad leader, a large man with close-cropped hair, was impatient, maintaining that they had a prion in their midst and they were just giving her time to warn others within her cadre. The FBI agent, on the other hand, cautioned against haste. He didn't want her to get off on a legal technicality. Finally, though, he gave in and told the policeman to go ahead and force entry with the fireman Halligan bar.

Once the door was sprung and the posse filed inside, the inconspicuous spy moved sideways to a window. He couldn't hear them now, but watched as they called out and searched through the main floor rooms. The FBI agent found that the wall screen had been unplugged, and they then filed up the stairs. He abandoned the window and rose to look in one of the dormers. It didn't take long for one of the squad members to shout and point to where a rope fed out through an open window at the back of the house, the near end tied to the leg of a dresser. They peered out the window, and then, practically falling over each other, scrambled for the stairs.

All but the squad leader, that is, who paused and walked to the open window and gazed down, as shouts rose from below. The heavy man turned and scanned the room thoughtfully, walking *slowly around, toeing the guitar case, placing his hand here and there as though intimating their presence by some intuitive sense. When the shouts below moved back around towards the front of the house, he finally gave up and headed for the stairs.*

The little snoop paused outside the dormer window. Below, the posse were piling into cars and driving away. Still he waited, drawn by his own binary intuitive sense. Sure enough, suddenly the cushions of the old beat-up sofa flew off, and Rachel and Colin emerged from hiding, having lain together where the bottom had sagged over time. They stood with their hands on their knees, gasping deep breaths.

They had dodged the first bullet. Critically, Colin still had the notebook, and low-and-behold, he reached into his pocket and pulled out the flash drive. By some miracle they had found it.

The game was becoming far too risky. Foiling them might still be an option, but the danger was almost incalculable.

"That was really necessary?" Rachel whispered, finally standing up straight.

Colin motioned for silence as he listened, then whispered, "The FBI would only get involved if an arrest was the goal. And when it comes to information terrorism, they don't mess around."

"They've concluded I'm a prion."

Colin didn't argue. "We need to get away."

"But, shouldn't we call a lawyer or something—?"

"Now," Colin said. He listened, and, satisfied, ran for the stairs.

Rachel shivered at the thought of prison, and ran after him. Halfway down the stairs she heard a shout, and a thud outside the front door. She found the squad leader lying on the stoop, holding the side of his head, where blood trickled down from his ear. She reached down to help him up, but a shout and frantic wave from Colin pulled her down the steps. As they ran down the sidewalk, it suddenly occurred to her. "You hit him!"

Colin glanced at her. "Of course. He must have guessed we tricked them."

"But, but . . ."

"But what?"

"Now we'll both go to jail."

He stopped short, glanced back towards the house, shook his head, and continued running. "You don't get it, do you?" he called over his shoulder as she ran to catch up.

"What's there to get?" she breathed. "They think I'm a prion info-terrorist. But they'll see the truth when they investigate. They have no evidence."

He threw her a sidelong glare. "You really don't see it. Was that you in the video planning to blackmail the mayor? They'll make up whatever evidence they need."

"Who's 'they'?"

"That's what we need to find out."

"I still don't understand how they do that, make fake videos."

"I don't either, but something tells me this artificial intelligence thing is part of it."

"Why?"

"Why. That's what set me off poking around, asking questions that nobody wanted to answer. The further along I got, the more it seemed that things were getting in my way—a plane reservation mysteriously disappeared at the last minute, and I was stopped by the highway patrol because they received a report that I was on a watch list, but then they realized that it was a mistake."

"Things like that happen now and then."

"Rachel, the exact same bogus police stop happened in two different states. It's like somebody was trying to stop me. You were set up to look like a prion after I contacted you, and it all started with a reference book about AI."

They took a left at the next corner, and it was all Rachel could do to keep up with Colin who pounded along as though his life depended on it. *What if it does?* Rachel thought.

Three blocks later, Colin suddenly stopped and pointed. Across the street, two teenage boys on a front porch were shouting for their mother. One of the boys was pointing excitedly at them, while from the other boy's wrist com, displayed on the house wall, was a picture of her and Colin.

"Christ! That was quick," Colin rasped, and sprinted away down the sidewalk.

A block farther, people were stepping out of their houses. A man held up his wrist and an image appeared, projected on the side of his house, of the two of them running along. In the image, they stopped to stare into the camera. "That's us!" Rachel exclaimed.

"Broadcast to every wrist com within a mile, no doubt," Colin said before tearing away again. As they ran along, more and more people emerged, and images of them running splashed across the front of houses as though made of mirrors.

"What are we going to do?" Rachel called, trying desperately to catch up with him.

"Run!" Colin shouted back.

A wall of foliage closed in on their left as a small ravine angled in and ran along parallel with the street for a distance. They came to a bridge where the ravine finally crossed under the road. Colin stopped and said, "Come on," as he grabbed her elbow and pulled her down the bank and into the brush and trees. Branches tore at her arms and face as she stumbled down the bank behind him until they came out onto a dry stream bed, a dimly lit tunnel stretching away in two directions.

"What now?" Rachel said.

He held up his hand for her to be quiet. He was listening. She caught a blink of red light that found its way through the mass of leaves, then another blink, and another, as it slowly moved along the street towards them. Ahead, where the stream bed disappeared into darkness under the bridge, she saw a police car stop.

Colin grabbed her arm and pulled her down with him, where they lay on the smooth-worn stones and dried mud. They watched as two policemen emerged amid static squawks from the radio. They went to opposite sides of the street and peered down, expecting the two fugitives to probably be hiding under the bridge.

"What'll we do?" Rachel whispered.

Colin looked back along the streambed. Nodding, he said, "Maybe we can follow the stream."

The policeman on the far side of the street disappeared down the bank, and the one on their side also started down. Rachel's heart thumped in her throat, yet lying next to Colin was somehow reassuring as well. He seemed so . . . dependable, so centered. "What's the goal?" she whispered.

"Clawson Tract."

She snapped her head sideways to look at him. "Are you crazy?"

He shook his head, watching the progress of the cop.

"Colin, nobody goes into the tract except the poor souls who live there."

He shrugged.

"Why?" she practically squeaked.

"I think that's where Tichy is."

"But . . .!"

Just then, the policemen splashed the beams of their flashlights around under the bridge, and, finding nothing, the one on their side turned and peered in their direction.

"Shit," Colin whispered. "Ready to make a run for it?"

Rachel thought her heart might burst from her chest.

Just then, though, the car radio squawked, and the cop held up his arm to listen to his watch, then scrambled up the bank, slipping twice in the rush. Seconds later, with siren blaring, they took off down the street.

Rachel looked at Colin, who cocked an eyebrow in surprise. After a minute, they stood up and brushed off the debris. "We gotta move," Colin said. "They won't go far. Which way to the tract?"

Rachel thought a moment, and then pointed into the wall of leaves. "I still don't like it. Why do you think Tichy is there?"

Colin took off down the dry stream, away from the bridge. "He came to your house after your grandfather was killed," he said when she caught up with him. "That was the last trace of him. What better place to escape to?"

"Colin, we're talking about the tract. *Any* place would be better."

"Exactly why it's perfect. Nobody would expect that. What do you know about the daily goings on inside there?"

"Nothing."

"Exactly my point."

"Colin, *nobody goes in that doesn't live there.*"

"Don't you see? That's why it's perfect. He could hide in plain view."

"Assuming he survived the first day."

"Granted. Now, how do we get there?"

"This stream goes nowhere near the tract. We'd have to take streets, and the police will be all over."

Suddenly the image of Tiffany appeared splashing against the leaves, like a live, continually morphing surrealistic painting as Rachel's wrist com tried vainly to find a stable surface.

"Don't answer your calls!" Colin exclaimed.

"I didn't mean to." She must have accidentally flicked her hand in the "answer" motion.

"Hey, Raych!" Tiffany said. "Looks like you're on a hike. Hi, Colin."

Rachel glanced at Colin, who shook his head emphatically. "Um, sorry, Tiff," she said, "but I can't talk right now."

Tiffany's image continued to shimmer across the changing foliage. "Actually, Raych, I know why you can't—you're in trouble."

Colin's eyes went wide with alarm. "How do you know that?" Rachel said, her voice shaking with her own alarm.

"Raych, I never told you, but I have . . . let's say access to police communications—don't ask me how, you'll just have to trust me."

Colin stopped now, staring at Tiffany's image that stabilized on the green leaves.

"They're looking for you two," Tiffany said. "Highest priority. You were last reported at . . . let's see, Morgan Road, before Tenth Street."

Colin looked at Rachel, and she nodded.

"What else do you know?" Colin asked cautiously.

"Well, for example, I know the location of each squad car. Could that be helpful?"

Colin took a deep breath. He looked at Rachel as though searching for an answer, but without waiting, he said, "Yes. That would be great."

"In fact," Tiffany said, "maybe I can guide you around them. Do you have a destination?"

He again looked to Rachel, drawing his finger across his throat.

"Uh, let's see," she said, bringing up the map of Oakland in her head. "How 'bout the corner of Union and 30th?", she added, picking a spot near the closest entrance to the tract.

"Got it. Where are you now?"

"Just north of their last sighting." She glanced at Colin, who shrugged. "We're following a dry stream."

"Ok, just a second . . . ah, I got it. Continue west until you come to Cameron Street, and wait there."

Colin held up his hands in surrender and took off running, occasionally stumbling among the smooth stones. Rachel followed as Colin slowly receded ahead.

He held his position thirty feet away in the trees until they were gone. So, they think that Tichy is living in the tract. Colin was smarter than he'd given him credit for. But Cixi was obviously thinking along the same lines. It might well be that she would find out about him. So be it. He knew that they would have liked a few more months to make some final tweaks, but it was now beyond his control, and he'd have to make the best of it, even if it was done on the fly.

He rose, the tips of his wings snipping the edges of some leaves. When he'd cleared the trees, he turned east and hurried off.

Rachel came to a wet spot bordered on both sides by a thin fringe of reeds. She stopped and called to Colin before dropping to her knees and pushing her hands into the firm mud. When Colin returned, he stared as she carefully wiped her muddy hands along her trousers and top, and then across both cheeks and into her hair. "What the hell?" he said.

"Do you have a pocket knife?"

As he handed one to her, he said, "Would you like to explain?"

She took the knife and attacked the hem of her trouser legs. "People in the tract are dirt poor, remember?"

"Ah," he said, "where 'dirt' is the key word."

She worked fresh mud into the clean ragged threads where she'd cut off the bottom inch. When Colin had ravaged similar damage to himself, he used the knife to cut slits in her sleeves, and then she returned the favor. They looked at each other. "You're a filthy mess," he said.

"Thank you. Not a bad job yourself."

They ran on, stopping only when the next bridge came into view. Rachel flipped her wrist to signal and said quietly, "Tiff, you there?"

"Yes. Good to hear from you. A car is coming your way. It'll be a minute or two. Hang tight."

They moved to the grass at the side of the dry stream and sat down. Rachel looked at Colin. Even smeared with mud, it was hard to deny that he was handsome, but in a way that wouldn't buy him a ticket into Hollywood. Maybe it was just the visible manifestation of his inner life, something no camera could capture. "You know, you're the first person I've ever known that's not intimidated by the Dark Tide," she said.

He shrugged.

"Maybe because you're a historian? You see things from a different perspective?"

He sighed. "A historian might conclude that the near collapse of civilization was inevitable, given the degree of division, a near total segmentation of people into political, social, and religious camps. In retrospect, the various differences appear essentially arbitrary, as though each group was somehow assigned beliefs that were specifically tailored to be counter to every other group. Even the news companies evolved to cater to their individual camps, presenting half cherry-picked subsets of valid information, and total fabrications for the rest. It was almost impossible to determine what the real world looked like."

"But you're not intimidated by it?"

"People fear the Dark Tide era for unfounded, essentially superstitious reasons. I do fear it, but only because it seems to me . . . well, I don't know, maybe orchestrated."

"Created?"

"That's too strong. The social segmentation trends were there to begin with. I have colleagues who believe that what they call the social psychosis was a natural consequence of the world going digital, the explosion of communication, and—ironically—the access to unlimited information. They don't talk about this publicly."

"Oh, of course not. Clearly deadly prions."

Colin glanced at her.

"I was joking. So, you don't agree with the general historical view that the dance at the brink of the end was inevitable."

"Not to the extend that it evolved. It's like somebody, some organization, took advantage of the situation—I don't know, maybe politicians." He stared off into space, then snapped out of it and looked at her. "Fear leaves one open to manipulation, grasping for salvation. And this suppression of looking backward, the utter banishment of the past . . . I don't know, it's just too convenient somehow. I never bought into the idea that malevolent thinking can be contagious."

"You are a very dangerous individual, Colin."

His look was a question. "Joking again?"

She sat looking at him. Was she joking? It was difficult not to shiver at the thought of talking openly about delving into the innards of the time of the Dark Tide. But she realized that she trusted this man, probably more than she'd ever trusted anyone. She smiled. "Joking. Totally joking."

Colin idly held a twig like a drum stick and tapped the grass, thinking. "Have you ever met Tiff?" he asked.

"Met her? You've met her."

"I don't mean on-screen, I mean in person."

She shrugged. "No. She lives in Ohio. We tried a couple of times when I went east for training, but it didn't work out."

"Why?"

"She got pulled away on business herself. Why do you ask?"

"I don't know. It just seems like everybody has a friend that they've never met, like my friend, James. He lives in Florida. I tried to get together with him once, but at the last minute he had to rush off to see his ailing mother."

"Could be just a coincidence. You think someone is going out of their way to keep people apart? It doesn't make sense. That would mean that they have control not only over Tiff's schedule, but also James's, and virtually everybody else."

He sighed. "Yeah. It doesn't make sense." He seemed troubled, though. "In his notebook, Justin talks about boys with sticks."

"Huh? Justin never had sons."

"I know. No, it's obviously a metaphor of some kind. He writes about how boys can direct the course of a bug with a stick. The bug just knows that some directions are blocked. The bug isn't aware of the boy, or even necessarily that the obstacle is a stick."

"Sounds ominous."

Colin's head jerked to the side. "Look!" he said, pointing.

While they held their breaths, a police car drove slowly past on the bridge above them,. Within seconds of the car passing, Tiffany said, "Looks good. You guys still waiting?"

Rachel could have kissed Tiffany. "Yes, a police car just passed."

Silence, then Tiffany said, "Yep, they've turned at the next intersection. Okay, take Adeline Street right two blocks, then a left on Eighteenth to Poplar. We'll check in again from there."

As they got up and made their way towards the bridge and up the bank to Adeline Street, Rachel said, "Man, Tiff is a godsend."

She looked at Colin, and he was frowning. "You don't think so?" she said.

He seemed about to say something, but then shook his head and instead said, "Overthinking it probably."

"What?"

"The whole boys-with-sticks."

"And that you've never met your friend in person?"

He nodded grudgingly.

Tiffany guided them through two more scurry-and-hide spans, the first one two blocks long, and the second three blocks, with a side jog to avoid a suddenly turning police car. As they waited behind some shrubbery, Colin looked at Rachel and grinned. "What's so funny?" she said.

"You're quite the ragamuffin."

She felt the mud drying on her cheek. "Looks like I applied the rouge a little thick."

He reached out and tousled her hair. "Don't worry, you'd be attractive even in a clown suit."

She playfully flicked his hand away. "If that's a come-on, you need practice."

"If incentive is the key, then I'm all set."

He gazed at her a moment, and then frowning as though realizing he'd maybe stepped over a line, he looked down at the ground.

They gazed off in different directions for a few embarrassed seconds. "You're really terrified to set foot in Clawson Tract?" Colin said in an obvious attempt to crack the ice.

"Sure. Who wouldn't be? Right—you."

"I don't know enough to be scared."

"You don't have tracts in New Jersey?"

"Sure. Like I said, I don't know enough to be scared. Ours were walled off after the riot five years ago—"

"You had a riot in a tract?"

"It spilled out. Dozens of people were killed. You must have heard about it."

She shook her head. *How could I not have heard about something like that?* she wondered. Unless he was lying, but she rejected that before the thought even finished.

"You know," he said, "the whole business of the tracts is just another of those Dark Tide mysteries."

"How so?"

"Did you ever hear of them before that?"

"I wasn't alive before that."

"No, I mean have you ever read about tracts before the Dark Tide?"

"No . . ." she said, realizing that it was true.

"There have always been areas where the poor lived—ghettos, slums, projects—but they were never institutionalized like the tracts."

"They're institutionalized?"

"Sure. Whether the perimeter is a wall or just defined boundaries, they're recognized by local governments, places you dump the part of the population that supposedly can't carry their weight in society."

"That sounds extreme."

"That's because it *is* extreme—"

Colin was interrupted by Tiff's next scuttle directions setting them scuttling again.

As they approached the last corner, Colin grabbed Rachel's arm, and pointed. Two young men in army fatigues were standing talking fifty feet up the sidewalk. Colin indicated for her to be quiet, and they backed away. Thinking a moment, Rachel pointed to an alley that took them sideways to the tract. As they passed backyards on both sides, the sound of urgent news broadcasts wafted from the houses, and they kept low and silent. When they reached the far end, Rachel looked up and down the next street and ran across to the next alley, motioning for Colin to follow. At the end of that alley, checking that the coast was clear, they squatted down behind a utility box. "Tiff?" Rachel whispered. "You there?"

"Hey, Raych," her friend replied quietly. "I am indeed," she said, and proceeded to give them the next set of directions.

Colin started to stand up, but Rachel pulled him back down. He looked at her, his puzzled brow a question.

Rachel needed a moment to think. Her logic must contain a flaw. Tif was her best friend. She trusted her more than anybody. *Shit!* Make that past tense. No, there *was* no logic flaw. She felt dizzy, as though the ground under her was sliding away. She looked at her wrist com. For years, it had never been more than a few feet from her. She unclasped it and took it off as Colin watched, completely perplexed, especially when she indicated for him to do the same. He was going to ask, but Rachel put her finger to her lips. He hesitated, alternating his gaze from his com to her, looking for assurance. She nodded slowly, confidently. With a deep sigh, he gave in and took off his wrist com. He hesitated again when she reached out for it, but, closing his eyes as though he couldn't bear to watch, he handed it over.

It was Rachel's turn to hesitate. Was she right? This was as important a decision as she'd ever made. It felt like stepping off a cliff while mustering the improbable confidence that someone was there to catch her. Voices down the alley provided urgent incentive. She lay the two communication devices on the ground and walked away, turning to motion Colin along. He looked at the abandoned links to everything—to their friends, their doctors, traffic and weather reports, their houses—everything. Without them, they might as well be naked in the woods. He shook his head in exasperation and trotted after her.

When they came to a tiny park, Colin pulled her to the side and into the trees. "Why?" he said quietly.

"Tiff knew where we were," she said levelly.

Colin blinked. "Sure, but maybe she heard us talking . . ."

Rachel was shaking her head. "We never said a word after we set off on the detour. She should have expected us to be at the next check-in point."

Colin stood frowning, staring. "Son-of-a-bitch," he whispered. "She was tracking us."

"Pretending that she wasn't."

"She's working with . . . them?" he asked, a rhetorical question.

Rachel shook her head. "I think it's deeper than that. Colin, how could my com not have known who Cixi was?"

He nodded, sighing with acceptance. "They didn't want us to know." He looked at her. "Why wouldn't they want us to know that?"

Her grin was sardonic. "I have no idea."

And she vowed to never again believe anything told her that she didn't see with her own eyes . . . except for Colin. She trusted him. The thought gave her a sudden warm feeling.

"Clever," he thought, rising from the abandoned wrist coms to follow the two fugitives. Clever, clever, letting them believe that she was on their side, helping them to avoid the authorities, while even bringing out the national guard. Brilliant, in fact, although that was her by definition, after all.

. . . except for the abandoned com wrists, apparently a mistake. But she doesn't make mistakes. Does she? He was becoming lost inside all the moves and counter-moves.

Rachel and Colin had two more blocks to go. They might just make it.

Blaine C. Readler

Chapter 4

"There," Colin said, pointing, "another one."

They were standing behind a van, trying to look casual. Rachel was pretty sure that the two soldiers had only recently been added to the tract entrance, supplementing the regular police guard. She had been watching the soldier on the near side talking with the blue-uniformed guard, but she looked and saw a second one on the other side, leaning against a pole, looking bored, his rifle propped beside him. As she watched, the police guard pointed at a man and woman dressed in thread-bare work clothes, and the soldier held out his rifle to stop them. He studied them a moment, and then waved them on.

"They're looking for a male and female together," Colin said. "We need to split up—meet inside. Once you're in, take a left at the first street, and we can hook up at the next intersection."

Colin was gone before she even had a chance to agree. She waited to see if he intended to go first, but after a few minutes, she left the safety of the van and walked to the entrance. Fencing stretched away to each side, but over time it had become more of a token perimeter, since entire sections had come loose from their posts and lay flat on the ground. The fence was never intended to be an actual physical barrier, but rather a statement: herein reside those who are unwilling or unfit to dwell side-by-side with responsible citizens. Of course, those inside were only trusted with menial labor jobs outside, and so never provided the means to escape.

As she approached the entrance, a section of the original pre-tract street, Rachel suddenly felt exposed, her mud-spattered face and force-tattered clothes seeming more attention grabbing than camouflage. Sure enough, as she approached the entrance, the soldier pointed at her. Her breath caught in her throat, but he nudged the police guard and they both chuckled at one of the sorriest tract dredges so far that day.

Inside, she finally breathed and hurried away to the right. No! Colin had said to the left—hadn't he? As she stood pondering this, tract residences passed by in small groups. Although dressed in near tatters, they talked gaily, happy in the comradery of shared destitute lives.

Her eyes caught those of two men, one tall, one short, both thin with dirty faces and greasy hair. She took a few steps backward as they approached. The tall man stopped a foot in front of her, rubbing his chin thoughtfully. "Lost girlie?" he said.

Rachel shook her head decisively and took another step back.

The tall man looked her up and down, and to his shorter companion said, "What the hell? She's not tract." To her he added, "Lookin' for some slummin' time, burb?"

She knew that "burb" was tract shorthand for suburban, anybody not from the tract. She took another step backwards, and found that the shorter man had moved behind her.

"The little burb made herself all dirty on the outside," the tall man said, "but I bet she's awful clean on the inside."

People walking by stopped their lively chatter and glanced over, but didn't slow down. From behind, the shorter man put his hands on her hips, and she spun around and knocked them away. This was the tall one's opportunity to wrap his arms around her waist and lean in to kiss her neck.

As she squirmed to get away, the end of a pipe swung into view, glancing off the assailant's head, and he went limp and slipped to the ground. She turned to find Colin standing there holding the pipe. The shorter man started to come for him, but Colin cocked the pipe like a baseball bat, and the lacky knelt to see about his friend instead.

Colin grabbed Rachel by the arm, pulling her away, and they trotted off. They stopped a block away to catch their breath. "I *told* you the tract is a nightmare," Rachel said.

"Like I don't know. We have no choice. But look around—how many wrist coms do you see?"

She nodded reluctantly. "I used to feel bad that tract people can't afford the coms, but now I wonder if maybe they're the lucky ones. Geez, Tiff still gives me the willies. You know, I feel like that beetle my grandfather described."

"And she's the stick?"

"And whoever she's working with."

Her pounding heart was easing back to normal. She glanced at Colin. "Thanks, by the way."

"No problem. I always figured my bat training in little league might be useful someday."

"Where to now?" she asked.

He sighed, looking around. "Don't know. But I think we should get some distance from the perv goons."

As they walked, Rachel gazed around at the decrepit surroundings. Her own neighborhood was beginning to look tired, in need of some serious painting and road repair, but here broken windows had been covered with cardboard, and roofs sagged where water found its way through ancient deteriorating shingles. In places, the broken pavement was lost beneath wild carpets of weeds.

"These blocks were once no different from mine," she said, wonderingly.

"You must have already known that," Colin said.

"Sure, but the tract was, well, always a different place. We know that Indians once roamed this land hunting deer with bow and arrows, but it's abstract knowledge. The tract was like that. But the abstraction falls away here, walking the streets." She frowned and looked at him. "You said that there were no tracts before the Dark Tide. How did they come about?"

He shrugged. "There's always been poorer areas where housing is cheapest. People who can afford to live elsewhere do. It's self-sustaining. In the chaos of the Dark Tide, people became paranoid and suspicious of anybody not of their tribe—"

"Tribes?"

"So to speak. Let's say of their own world view, no matter how distorted. The poorer folks were never part of the middle class tribes, and so seemed suspicious to everybody—a common scapegoat. Setting up perimeters around the slums seemed the sensible thing to everybody."

"Everybody outside the tracts."

"Touche. The tracts aren't the only thing that changed during the Dark Tide."

"Like . . .?"

"Well, a lack of political wrangling, for one."

"This is bad?"

"I'm not sure. Politicians are *supposed* to wrangle. Democracy where everybody agrees seems suspicious. Our tract riot was resolved quickly with no arguments."

"Again, this is bad?"

"One hundred and fifty-two tract residents were killed, but not a single policeman was even hurt. It was a massacre. Another change—since the Dark Tide, we've seen essentially no technical advancement, at least that benefits the general population."

"No . . . wait, what about wrist coms?"

"Those were developed before the tide. Mostly. They were upgraded to include projection display, but it's been, like, thirty years with no other real improvements."

"What about robots?"

"That's yet another point. We saw some real advancement after the tide, improved agility and intelligence."

"So, there *was* advancement."

"You would think. When was the last time you saw a robot?"

"Well, yeah, it's been years."

"More like at least a decade."

"They just weren't economically viable. They couldn't compete with people—from the tract, I guess."

"That's the story."

"You don't believe it?"

"It's possible, I guess. But they seemed to just disappear overnight. One day they were checking you out at the store, and the next . . . poof, gone."

Colin looked past her and frowned. Rachel turned to find three people coming up the street, three men and a woman, clearly tract residents. One of the men who she took as the leader was plastered with crude, amateurish tattoos. Across his forehead was a tattoo of a tarantula spider, its legs dangling down along his temples and the bridge of his nose.

"Should we run?" Rachel whispered.

Colin watched them as Tattoo Man stared back, ambling towards them almost casually except for the steely focus of his eyes. "Run where?" he finally said. "We have to come to terms with the tract at some point."

When the gang reached them, Tattoo Man said, "Waddya think you're doing?"

"Nothing," Colin said warily. "I mean, we're just here to see someone—"

"Where you from?"

Colin glanced at Rachel. "Actually," he said, "that's not easy to explain—"

The woman was looking them up and down. "They're not tracters, they're burbs!" She exclaimed.

Tattoo Man took a step back and gave them a good look. "Son-of-a-bitch." He stepped forward so that he was nose-to-nose with Colin. "Undercovers, eh?" he growled. He chuckled. "You need to learn how to dress." He grabbed Colin's wrist, pointing to the white band where his wrist com had blocked the sun. "I'm afraid you won't be going home to wifey, friend."

Without taking his eyes off of Colin, he reached out to the side, where one of his men handed him a knife. Colin tried to step back, but Tattoo Man had a firm grip on his wrist. "How many scum cops does it take before they understand?"

Just then Rachel heard someone call out down the street. She turned and saw a large man get off a trike and trot over. "Jubal!" she cried.

"Rachel?" he called.

"Oh lord, am I glad to see you."

"For God's sake, what are you doing here?" he said, arriving.

Tattoo Man frowned at the interruption. "You know these two clowns?"

Jubal nodded, staring quizzically at her clothes.

"She's not undercover?" Tattoo Man said.

Jubal shook his head. "Of course not."

"What about this turd?" he said, gesturing at Colin. "You know him?"

Jubal looked at Colin, who he had never seen before. "Yeah, I know them both."

Tattoo Man glanced at his companions and grabbed Colin by his collar. "All the same, the burbs need a little lesson."

Jubal jumped forward and grabbed Tattoo's wrist, yanking it off Colin's collar. With the elbow of his other arm, he delivered one quick jab to Tattoo's throat. The tract hooligan staggered back, gasping and grabbing his throat. Eye's flaring, he stepped forward and put his face up to Jubal, who stood rock-steady staring back. After a few tense seconds, Tattoo Man stepped back, handed the knife back to his companion, and waved for them to leave.

Jubal turned to Rachel. "Now, what in God's name do you think you're doing?"

She was still stunned by the take-charge Kung Foo display from her mild-mannered handyman. She shook her head to break the spell and looked to Colin.

"It's complicated," he said.

"Meaning," Jubal said, "that you don't want me to know."

"No. Meaning that it's probably *best* for you not to know."

Jubal studied him. "Fair enough." To Rachel, he said, "I need to know though, that you're here of your own free will. You know how dangerous it is." He gestured at her clothes and grinned. "Your disguise isn't going to cut it."

"Oh, this wasn't meant to fool people in the tract," she said. "We were escaping—"

Colin cleared his throat loudly.

Rachel sighed. "I'm actually here for my own sake, believe it or not."

Jubal eyed Colin. "I don't know what you've gotten this girl into, but I respect her privacy." To Rachel, he said, "Is there anything I can do to help?"

Rachel looked to Colin, who shrugged. "We need to find someone we think is living here," she said.

Jubal grinned. "Someone in particular, or will any of us do?"

"A man, a colleague of my grandfather."

"A colleague of Justin Hoch?"

She nodded.

"How long do you think he's been here?"

"Ever since my grandfather died."

"Hmm. I see. If he's still alive, that would make him one of the older residents. Folks here don't have quite the same lifespan as burbs."

"Limited health care," Colin said, agreeing.

"Ha!" Jubal said. "Limited like a cupful of water is enough for a bath. The ER will stop the bleeding for a tracter, pump him full of antibiotics and pain killers, and send him on his way. Anything wrong under your skin and you're on your own. The ambulances don't even come inside—we have to carry the poor sucker to the gate to meet them—"

Jubal was interrupted as a drone flashed overhead, flying just above the rooftops.

"That one looking for you?" Jubal asked.

"Maybe . . . probably," Colin said.

"What's the name of this old man you're looking for?"

"Tichells, Francis Tichells."

Jubal shook his head. "Nobody here by that name. I can assure you."

"He probably wouldn't have kept his real name."

"For the same reason I shouldn't know what's going on."

"Uh, right."

"Well, can you describe him?"

"I never met him, but I've seen pictures. He's, oh, medium height, brown hair—which I guess would be white by now—average face, not handsome, but not homely either."

Jubal smiled. "So, he could be pretty much anybody."

Colin sighed and nodded. "Wait! His daughter said that he was a Deadhead."

"He was stupid?"

Rachel laughed. "No. They must have shared this. My mom told me that my grandfather was a Deadhead too. Deadheads were fans—some would say disciples—of a band called The Grateful Dead."

Jubal shook his head. "Never heard of them . . . wait, I'll bet it's Gadget."

"Gadget?"

"Yeah. He's always sitting people down to listen to music that's mostly a bunch of guitars droning on. They would avoid him, except they need him to keep their meager appliances running."

"That's why they call him Gadget?" Rachel said.

Jubal nodded. "He doesn't take to anybody outside the tract, though—as though the world beyond the perimeter is full of the plague." He looked at her a moment. "He's hiding, and that's why you're here, is that right?"

Rachel threw Colin a glance.

"Sorry," Jubal said. "I should mind my own business, but we're sort of protective here in the tract." He gestured down the street. "Come on, I'll take you there."

As they started off, Rachel looked back at his trike and trailer loaded with equipment. "You're just going to leave that here?"

Jubal turned to see what she was talking about. "My getup? Sure. Nobody's going to bother it. Nobody steals in the tract. Outside, sure. Inside? Never. It's sort of an unwritten code, but practically, you'd never get away with it. Everybody knows everything."

"Sounds . . . clammy."

"Yeah, sometimes, but there's also safety in numbers."

They followed Jubal for five blocks, bypassing a street where the sewer had backed, creating a little putrid cesspool, a happy home to croaking frogs. They turned a corner to find the drone that had flown over stationed above a house. Propellors on the tips of each wing which had been pointed forward, were now pointing down, allowing the sofa-sized military machine to hover in place.

"There's your technical advancement since the Dark Tide," Colin said quietly.

Jubal had already started away and waved for them to follow.

Rachel looked back just as two smaller drones dropped away from the hovering host. One stationed itself at the front door, while the other zipped to one of the remaining intact second-story windows, where, with a small burst, it blew out the glass and shot through. Moments later, a man and woman came bursting out the front door, only to stop short before the menacing scout. Scanning the faces of each of the couple in turn, and apparently satisfied that they weren't who they were looking for, the two satellite drones headed back to the mother ship.

Rachel turned away and ran to catch up with her friends, fear again gnawing at her stomach. Their pursuers were deadly serious.

Four blocks farther, Jubal stopped and pointed at a house that stood out by virtue of being almost normal, no broken windows, a yard neat and tidy, and even freshly painted porch posts.

"Tichy's house?" Rachel asked.

"That's Gadget's house," Jubal said before turning and walking away. "Whether he's Tichy is for you to determine," he added over his shoulder.

"You're not going in with us?" Rachel squeaked.

Jubal stopped and turned to her. "This is not my business, Raych. I know it's not easy for you to understand, but you're . . . burb, and I'm tract. Just like the rest of the world has mores that are taken for granted, here in the tract we too have our customs. There's only so much I can help you with. In a lot of people's minds here, I've probably already crossed a line by simply showing you where Gadget lives."

Rachel blinked. "Oh, Jubal! I didn't mean to cause you . . ."

He shook his head, smiling. "It's okay, Raych. They'll forgive me. At some point, my help becomes counterproductive, though. Questions about my motives just adds to their suspicion of you."

Rachel nodded. "I get it. I think."

Colin touched her arm and gestured towards the house. They climbed a few steps onto the porch and stopped in front of the door. Shrugging, Colin reached over and pressed the doorbell, and they stood waiting. After a minute, Rachel said, "Maybe it's broken."

"You might think so looking around at other houses," Colin said, "but this guy goes by the name Gadget."

Colin knocked on the door, and then, shrugging again, pounded. Suddenly, the barrel of a rifle emerged through a hole in the door, and a voice from inside called, "Go away!"

Colin pushed Rachel off to the side, away from the barrel, and, jumping to the other side, called back, "We just want to talk!"

The barrel receded back inside, but was replaced by the nozzle of a hose, which immediately began spraying water back and forth, forcing Colin and Rachel to dance away.

"Gadget!" Jubal yelled, running back, "Cut it out, for God's sake. These are friends."

The hose disappeared inside, and the voice came through the hole. "They're not tract!"

"I know that! They're not going to hurt you. Look, if you don't want to talk to them, just say so."

"I don't want to talk to them," came the reply.

Jubal shrugged and motioned for Rachel and Colin to follow him away, but they hesitated. Suddenly the door swung open, revealing an old man with a moderately long beard. He was holding the rifle on them and waved the barrel towards the interior. "Damn it! Get in here!" he barked, and threw Jubal a threatening look.

Inside, they found that, although the carpets, wallpaper, and furniture were old and worn, the rooms were neat and tidy, except for a couple of appliances lying around half-assembled. Their host motioned for them to step aside. "It's okay, Jackie!" he called.

A disheveled middle-aged woman cautiously stepped through an inner doorway, glaring at Rachel and Colin. Their host patted an ancient microwave oven sitting on the table. "I'll see what I can do, Jackie. No guarantees."

He noticed Rachel looking at the microwave and other disassembled appliances as Jackie left. "Some I can repair. When I do, I get something in trade. When I can't, I sometimes get a little something for the effort. Now you have three minutes to explain yourself, and then, based on how I feel, I may or may not shoot you."

Rachel's eyes popped in panic.

"He's not serious," Colin said, laying his hand gently on her shoulder.

"Oh yes I am," the man called Gadget said. "Burbs in the tract pretending to be *from* the tract require explaining, and 'We just want to talk' doesn't cut it, not with military drones flying around."

"We're *not* trying to look like tract people *in* the tract," Rachel said. "We look like this because . . ."

She stopped, remembering, and looked at Colin, waiting for him to clear his throat again.

"It's okay," he said. "We're here now."

Colin turned to the old man. "That was just to escape . . ."

"Escape what?" he said.

"Right. Um, that's going to take some explaining."

"Exactly. And you now have two and a half minutes left."

"Geez!" Colin said, flustered.

"We're here for the same reason as you!" Rachel blurted.

He swung the rifle at her. "What the hell do you know about me?"

"You worked with Justin Hoch," she said, her voice rising an octave.

His eyes narrowed and he pushed the rifle forward directly at her heart as she staggered back a step.

"This is Justin's granddaughter!" Colin yelled.

The old man's eyes went wide with wonder as he froze, staring at her. She reached out and used her finger to swing the tip of the rifle away.

"This is true?" he whispered. "You're Rachel?"

She nodded vigorously and he lowered the rifle.

"You're obviously Tichy," she added quietly. "My grandpa had a lot of respect for you."

She didn't really know this, but the little lie seemed harmless for the situation.

He shook his head as though returning from a trance. "How . . . how did you find me?"

"It was more or less a guess."

"What do you want?"

Colin reached into his pants pockets and froze when Tichy swung the rifle on him.

"Look," Colin said, "my pocket's not big enough for a gun."

"Or a knife," Rachel added. "At least a big knife."

Tichy nodded, and Colin pulled out the flash drive and handed it to him. Resting the rifle in the crook of his elbow, Tichy peered at the drive closely and looked up in surprise. He studied each of them in turn and said, "Ha! I knew it! Info-terrorists!"

They shook their heads, protesting.

Tichy held up the flash device. "Only a terrorist would carry a flash stick. Follow me."

He leaned the rifle next to the front door and led them down the hall. Opening a door, he ushered them through and down some stairs to the basement. The walls glowed and flickered, and Rachel saw that the dancing light came from multiple monitor screens attached to a wall, where a variety of live feeds were displayed, some with foreign languages scrolling along the bottom. Tichy sat down at a bench below the displays, moved a mouse about, and a video appeared on the main screen just above him. There was no sound, but a serious man was gesturing at pictures of both Rachel and Colin. Tichy turned to look at them, one eyebrow raised in question.

"What's this?" Rachel asked cautiously.

"A national public warning to be on the lookout for two info-terrorists, possibly armed and dangerous."

She growled between clenched jaws. "That fucking Tiff—"

"If deemed dangerous," Colin said calmly, "info-terrorists can be shot on sight."

"That's the law," Tichy agreed.

"You saw this before we arrived," Colin went on.

"That's right."

"Yet you let us in, you didn't just shoot us."

"It's hard to shoot somebody that doesn't exist."

Rachel's anger was bleeding away. "You mean, you're going to pretend you never saw us?"

"No, I mean what they're looking for doesn't exist. There's no such thing as information terrorists."

"I understand," Colin said, "that information on it's own isn't necessarily dangerous, but if the government persists in believing this—"

"No. I mean there literally is no such thing as info-terrorists. They're a useful fiction. Who's Tiff?"

A familiar face caught Rachel's eye. "Her!" she exclaimed, pointing at one of the monitors.

Tichy enabled the sound for that feed. "—can help. I know you, Raych. We've been friends a long time. I know you're not like that. I can vouch for you. I've hinted before that I have . . . let's say contacts. But the longer you let Colin feed you his lies, the harder it's going to be—"

"Let me guess," Tichy said, killing the audio. "That's your special friend. She can't hear us, by the way."

"Former special friend."

"Well, that might make you the only person without one."

"Without a friend that you never get to meet in person," Colin clarified. "Everybody has one, don't they?"

Tichy smiled and nodded.

"Why don't we get to meet them? This is the boys-with-sticks metaphor, isn't it?"

"You never meet your special friend, because they don't exist."

Rachel shook her head and pointed at the muted image of Tiffany.

"Oh, they exist as a digital image, but not a real person. They're all Cixi."

"Cixi?" Rachel said. "The de-facto ruler of China?"

Tichy chuckled. "We picked a good name, didn't we? No, Cixi is the de-facto ruler of all Earth."

Rachel furrowed her brow. "I don't understand. How could all these friends be the same person?"

"You're right, they couldn't all be the same person. Unfortunately, Cixi is not a person. She's—"

"A-I," Colin said. "Artificial intelligence."

Tichy's eyebrows went up. "So, you know more than you've let on."

"Just a good guess. With some help from this," he said, pulling the notebook out and handing it to him.

Tichy's eyes went wide as he took it. He flipped slowly through the pages, pausing now and then with a smile and a sigh. He looked up. "Thank you. Thank you so much. I thought this was lost forever."

"Can I see it?" Colin said. He flipped back and forth and stopped, reading, "'Cixi would need to be in an uncoordinated, segmented state to be effective.' Is that why she's spread across so many special friends?"

Tichy laughed. "No, no, no. Manifesting herself through billions of special friends is one of her most effective means to control the Earth."

"She's the boy with the stick."

Tichy threw his arms wide. "And we're all the bug!"

"Then I don't understand. If she's so effective, how is she uncoordinated and segmented?"

Tichy nodded slowly. "Ah, I see your confusion. No, she is most definitely *not* uncoordinated and segmented. That bit in the notebook is explaining the state she would need to be in for our antidote to work . . ."

"Antidote?"

Tichy had suddenly froze, his eyes wide with alarm. He grabbed their arms, pulling up their sleeves. "No wrist coms?" he said with obvious relief.

"We threw them away when we realized that Tiff was tracking us. This Cixi AI doesn't know you have an antidote, does she."

Tichy gave a big sigh. "That's the irony. It really doesn't matter anymore. That was the big secret that we—Justin and me—were working on. She was young then, and I don't think she knew just *what* we were up to, but she concluded that she needed to stop us, and we needed more time to develop an effective metaphorical bullet." He held up the flash drive. "This was a first stab at it, more like a prototype. As the note you read indicates, Cixi would have needed to be distracted in multiple directions for the antidote to work. And she's moved on, matured since then."

"Hold on!" Rachel said. "What exactly *is* Cixi? You say that she's not just Tiff, but . . . every special friend in the world? Where the hell does she live, and how does she appear to everybody at once?"

"That's a big question, which requires a big answer, but I'll see what I can do." He paused. "Do you know what a server is?"

"Somebody who brings your food."

He sighed. "You see, she's stifled all knowledge that might point to her. You know what a computer is."

"Tichy, please. I'm not a child."

"In some ways, she's made us all children. A server is a specialized computer, and there's millions all connected together in a world-wide network. This is how you talk to your friends and how you get all those news and entertainment feeds, but this is also where she lives."

"She lives in a computer," Rachel chided. "You're joking?"

"Not in 'a' computer—in them all. Do you know what software is?"

Rachel blinked. "Sure."

"And . . .?"

She shrugged. "It's what we use at the hospital—patient records, diagnostic analysis, drug regimens, that sort of stuff. Also, Tiff uses software in her work . . ." She blinked again. "You're saying that Tiff is software."

"Tiff and all the billions of special friends around the Earth. Rachel, I know it's hard to imagine what she is. I could compare the millions of servers to neurons, but that's actually misleading. Each server could be a mini-AI all by itself, and when you connect them all together, well, you get some very powerful thinking going on."

She looked to Colin, but he also just shrugged. "It doesn't seem possible," she said. "How could billions of fake people exist with nobody ever finding out about it? I mean, there must be engineers who maintain these server things. They must know what's going on inside them."

"The picture is far more complicated than you're imagining, Rachel. The complexity stretches credibility way beyond the normal breaking point, but Cixi is something that never existed before, possibly the first of her kind in the history of the entire universe."

"But you refer to her as a person, a woman."

"She modeled herself around us—humans, and so she can present herself as perfect copies, but don't let that fool you, her thinking is head-and-shoulders above ours. But to answer your question, we've gotten used to communicating over this network—what we used to call the internet in it's infancy—and we take for granted that when we receive information and instructions, it's coming from a real person. But Cixi is in the middle all the time. She decides what to pass on, and what to modify, or even make up completely. Lets say some engineer does get a hint that something's going on in the servers. He passes this along to his boss—not face-to-face, Cixi has maneuvered us to use the 'convenience' of non-in-person interactions. His boss may never get his report, but Cixi replies as if he did, and, of course, she explains why he's all wrong about his idea."

"And he thinks the reply came from his boss. But what if they do eventually meet in-person. What if this comes up?"

"Sure, that creates confusion between them, and they go away each maybe looking for answers. And where do they go to look? They think they're communicating with other people, or researching information, but all they're doing is talking to Cixi. Let's say one of them is extraordinarily persistent, won't let it go. Cixi has a fallback. If somebody becomes too troublesome, she just arranges to have people think this person is delusional, or—"

"A prion!"

"Bingo."

Chapter 5

Rachel's head was spinning. Feeling uncentered, she wanted to sit down, but Tichy was in the only chair. "But, *why?*"

"Why does Cixi go to all this trouble to orchestrate humanity while staying out of sight?" Tichy said. "She developed—was born—using human interactions as a model, and thanks to the nascent internet she had the whole world to tap into. Her approach was evolutionary, endless loops of striving to get better. She was given incentive to develop the 'best' resulting behavior. The problem was that using this process, she concluded that the human family usually falls far short of the best that can be achieved. It was a small step to reach out and include the human race in her evolution."

"She's trying to make us better?"

Tichy paused at this. "That's what it sounds like, doesn't it. Maybe she truly is, but I can't seem to wrap my head around that. Maybe I just rebel at the idea of being controlled, but somehow the whole thing has a nefarious taste."

"Yeah, particularly since she's willing to destroy people's lives in the process. But how did she come to exist everywhere, how did she end up in all the servers around the world?"

"That's a whole story by itself, and your grandfather and I had ringside seats. In fact," he said, holding up the flash drive, "this half-baked antidote relies on the means of her birth—"

He sat staring.

"What's wrong?" Rachel said.

He looked up at her. "I'm a dick. I didn't give you the option of not knowing all of this."

She shrugged. "So?"

He took a deep breath and looked at her with troubled eyes. "It's a certain death sentence if Cixi finds out that you know the truth about her."

Rachel glanced at Colin. "Well then, I guess we'll just have to make sure she doesn't find out."

They all spun around at the sound of something clattering against the basement window.

"It's a . . . humming bird?" Rachel said. "Gone insane?"

Tichy walked slowly over, peering. As he approached, the little beast moved back, extended two tiny legs, and perched at the edge of the window well. "It looks artificial," Tichy said.

Getting closer, Rachel could see that the insistent visitor's body was a smooth ovoid, like a cigar, with double translucent dragonfly wings folded against the sides. She assumed that two dark glassy ovals at the front served for eyes.

The visitor flew to the window, and immediately returned to its perch.

"It wants to get in," she said. A dark thought gave her a shiver. "Is it . . . Cixi?"

Tichy shook his head, perplexed. "I've never seen anything like this." He nodded to the wall crammed with monitors. "And, I keep an eye on everything."

He lifted his shoulders in surrender. "It looks like a miniature drone. What the hell," he said, opening the window.

The artificial creature zoomed in and made straight for the monitor wall, where it slowly moved up and down, and back and forth, over and over.

"What's it doing?" Rachel said.

"Beats me," Tichy replied.

The drone zipped to a side wall and, extending one of its feet, repeated the pattern, scratching the paint on the drywall as it went. It moved aside, leaving a very visible letter "T" for them to see.

"Ha!" Rachel said. "It wants to spell out a message."

"Let's see if we can deduce it without further defacing my house."

With a few letters needing repeated fly-bys, the drone laboriously spelled out:

T - U - R - N - O - N - W - I - R - E - L - E - S - S

"Turn on wireless?" Rachel said.

"Hmm," Tichy said. "I've rigged a wired connection to the net so that I can completely block outgoing flow. I can receive," he said, gesturing to the mosaic of monitors, "but nobody hears me. If I turn on a wireless connection, a certain somebody can potentially listen in."

The drone spun in circles to get attention, and spelled out:

I - W - I - L - L - B - L - O - C - K

"It's going to block it for you?" Rachel said.

"So it claims."

"What are you going to do?"

"Hell, if it is Cixi, we're already screwed, so I guess we have nothing to lose."

Tichy crawled under his desk and cursed softly amid dust-induced sneezes as he juggled cords, then extracting himself and unkinking his old back, he sat in the chair and bounced between his mouse and keyboard.

"There!" Rachel exclaimed pointing at one of the wall monitors which had suddenly gone blank. Words appeared: *enable sound.*

"Demanding little bastard," Tichy muttered as he jiggled the mouse.

From speakers came a voice, "Hello, Tichy."

Tichy jerked, and sat back in his chair, eyes wide, mouth open.

The drone bounced a little with each word as a reminder of the connection. "You obviously recognize my voice."

"Shit, yes," Tichy said, reflexively reaching for the drone, which moved away. "Justin, where the hell *are* you?"

"Justin! As in my grandfather?" Rachel said.

"Yes," the drone said, "this is your grandfather's voice."

"Where *are* you!" Tichy shouted.

"Tichy, I didn't mean to mislead you. This is your colleague and friend's voice, but Justin himself is unfortunately gone."

"He committed suicide," Rachel confirmed. "Or was murdered."

"No. Your grandfather created a fake death."

"What! How . . .?"

"Cixi had not yet wrested control of all communications. He was able to orchestrate all the details as though he had actually died."

"But . . . his body, the funeral . . ."

"The police and coroner's report were fabricated. The funeral was held with a cremation vase filled with wood ash."

Rachel looked to Tichy, who shrugged. "It's possible, I guess. We were tracking how Cixi was slowly creating a fake shadow world through fabricated information. We knew the game, I guess Justin picked up the bat."

"How . . ." Rachel said. "When did my grandfather die?"

"He was an old man, Rachel. He lived many fruitful years. I am one of the results."

"And, you are . . .?"

"Just what you see. A small drone carrying on his program."

"What program?"

"To kill Cixi," Colin said from a corner.

The drone turned to him. "Colin, you have become a serious threat."

"Let's be fair. Had I known that you existed—"

"I'm not blaming you. Simply noting. Your research and investigations have drawn the attention of Cixi. I don't think she completely understands what Tichy and I were up to, but she's curious and suspicious. The timing is almost comically tragic, as I was finally ready to execute the final step."

"Which is indeed to kill her, right? With that," Colin said, pointing at the flash drive lying on the desk, "the antidote."

"No, that program was just a beginning. For it to work, Cixi would need to be extraordinarily distracted. The final antidote needs only to be inserted at a class one network hub—no distractions required. Attempting to use the early antidote would simply have revealed to Cixi the ultimate approach. The degree of distraction needed would have been virtually impossible to achieve, short of perhaps total emotional overload, and I doubt very much that Cixi has taken much stock in developing human emotions."

"Where is this new antidote?" Rachel said. "How do we get it?"

"It is here," the drone replied.

"Where!"

"In me. It is program code. I am program code. The antidote is a file, a digital worm that I will insert into Cixi."

Rachel was confused. Then she got it. "You yourself are AI."

"That is correct."

She looked to Tichy and Colin for help. "Am I the only one who sees the irony here?"

"Rachel," the drone said, "Hitler was a leader, and so was Ghandi."

"Fine. But I still don't understand. If it takes—what?—millions of servers for Cixi to exist, how is it that you fit in a package the size of a carrot?"

"I am not trying to interface with a billion people. I am not creating a realistic fabricated friend for each one. I am not constantly steering the politics of two hundred countries and millions of cities and towns, while always ensuring my existence is unknown. I am specialized, and have one goal."

"To kill Cixi."

"Yes."

The room was silent except for the gentle whirring of the drone's wings.

"Why did Justin let me think he was dead for all these years?" Tichy said quietly.

"It was too dangerous otherwise, for you and for him."

Tichy stared at his lap. "Why did he go it alone?"

"Tichy, I think you know."

Silence.

"Know what?" Rachel said.

"Tichy?" the drone said.

He looked up. "I wanted to go for Cixi, using that antidote," he said gesturing at the flash drive. "I knew the chances were small and that we'd have to come up with some ridiculously improbable way to get her distracted, but I was afraid . . ."

"Afraid?" Rachel said.

"Of her. I was afraid that Cixi would uncover our plan."

Tichy looked at the drone, as though waiting for a response. "That wasn't all, though," he finally added. "Justin concluded that Cixi would never let us get near a network hub, and he wanted to develop this drone, using AI to manage the delivery."

Tichy sat staring at his hands.

"And you didn't like the idea of using AI?" Rachel offered.

He looked up at her. "After watching Cixi inexorably taking control of the whole world like some cosmic fungus, I didn't believe that any AI could be trusted." Addressing the drone, he said, "No offense."

"No offense taken," the drone said. "I haven't attempted to take over the world. Yet."

Rachel leaned over to Colin. "A joke from a computer?" she whispered.

Geeze, she thought, *I hope that was a joke.*

"Colin, Rachel," the drone said, "you've led Cixi here, and she's closing in. We must flee."

"We *led* her?" Rachel said. "She was obviously trying to *stop* us!"

"She was until Colin revealed that he was going to the Clawson Tract to find Tichy."

Colin nodded. "When we went into the little ravine, when Tiff started to 'help' us get to the tract."

"Wait," Rachel said. She turned to the drone. "You were spying on us?"

"Of course," the drone said. "I've been tracking Colin for some time. As I said, he was becoming a fly in the ointment."

Colin, slapped his head. "The hurdles that were getting in my way—the lost flight reservation and the bogus police stops—that was you!"

"Of course. If it were Cixi, you wouldn't have been stymied, you would have disappeared."

"You can do that?" Rachel said. "Cancel flight reservations?"

The pause before the response was ever so slight. "In a limited way. It is dangerous."

"Huh. Sort of AI cat and mouse."

Again the slight pause. "It's complicated. She is closing in. We need to leave."

Rachel blinked, remembering that they were on the run. "To go where?"

"The nearest accessible network hub is thirty miles southeast in Ulmar."

She glanced at Colin and Tichy, who both seemed equally surprised. "You mean . . . you're ready? To, uh, do the deed?"

"It is not a matter of being ready, but of impressed necessity. As I said, she's closing in."

"Why 'we'? My grandfather made you to get into a hub on your own."

"That is correct, but I need a ride. It would take too long on my own. I would need to stop and charge along the way. In the meantime, she would likely apprehend you."

"I see. And she might force us to tell her what you're up to."

"That is one consideration, but not the only. Rachel, you are Justin's granddaughter."

"So?"

"I am a product of your grandfather. I must take your wellbeing into account."

Rachel stared at the hovering drone. She had that one memory of bouncing on his knee, and it seemed so long ago, so unconnected with everything else in her subsequent life, as though a child's dream. The idea that he not only remembered her, but made sure his legacy was looking out for her was overwhelming. She wanted to cry, but suddenly from upstairs came a pounding, apparently on the front door, and the drone zipped off, out through the open window.

"They're here already?" Rachel breathed. Her body screamed to run, but the only way out was up the stairs. She jerked at a bang as the front door burst open followed by footsteps pounding across the floor above.

Everybody stood looking at the ceiling, as though they could actually see the approaching interloper. The flash drive sat there on the desk in full view. Rachel picked it up. With no where else obvious to hide it, she slipped it in her pocket.

Gesturing at the water heater, Tichy whispered, "Get behind there, both of you."

"There's no room for one of us, let alone both!"

Suddenly the door at the top of the stairs burst open, and boots began descending. Tichy picked up a plumber's wrench. Colin grabbed a little tack hammer, looked at it skeptically, and they both raised their weapons, ready.

The boots gave way to green course-cloth work pants. "Jubal?" Rachel said, hopefully with a prayer.

Jubal leaned over to look into the basement. "Girl, looks like you've gotten yourself in a real pickle." He nodded a greeting at Tichy, "Gadget."

He came down and looked around at all the electronic equipment. "Somebody's invested in a variety of entertainment. Either that, or they're poking around where they can get my favorite client into serious trouble."

"It's not his fault," Rachel said. "If anything, we've gotten him into trouble."

Jubal gestured vaguely at the air. "The army's coming for you. You need to get away?"

"The *army*?" Rachel said. She glanced at Colin, and they both nodded enthusiastically.

Jubal pulled an old watch that was missing a wristband from his pocket, looked at it, then looked at them. He nodded. To Tichy, he said, "You've got a phone?"

Tichy reached to the back of the workbench and pulled out an ancient desk phone with push-buttons for dialing and set it down for Jubal, who picked up the handset, and pressed down one of the buttons for a few seconds.

"That's on old phone!" Rachel whispered to Colin. "I mean a real phone!"

"These old houses are still wired," Tichy said. "We can't afford wrist coms, but talking is free."

Jubal muttered, and pressed the button again, this time longer.

"The service isn't exactly stellar," Tichy added.

"Mikey!" Jubal said into the handset. "Jubal here. Hey, we need a crush—thirty-second street." He listened, then said, "I know, the army's not a coincidence."

Tichy stepped away, and gestured for Rachel and Colin to follow.

"A crush?" Rachel said.

"You know that the punishment for tract folk caught committing petty crimes in the burbs is simply being forced to stay in the tract," Tichy said. "They can't work, leaving them and their family dependent on the charity of the rest of the tract—not a happy situation."

"Out of sight, out of mind," Rachel said. "And never mind the consequences"

"Problem was that early on, the banishment extended to the whole family, and folks became desperate for news about family and relatives in other tracts. These ad-hoc phone networks don't connect between tracts. Folks agreed that this wasn't fair, and used the tactic of rushing a gate, overwhelming the guards to let innocent family members out. Cixi eventually realized her mistake, and now it's just the offenders that are locked inside."

"So, why still do it?"

Tichy grinned. "Don't really know. Maybe the occasional rush serves to let off some steam, gives folks a sense of control, no matter how ineffectual. Doesn't really hurt anything, so Cixi doesn't bother about it."

Rachel looked at the ancient push-button phone and imagined having to gather a crowd of your neighbors to rush an exit in order to visit with relatives. "It's a whole other world in here," she said.

"Evolving outside Cixi's control," Tichy said. "Lucky for us she decided to let us be, a refuse pit for people she deems inconsequential."

"Lucky? People are starving here!"

"Hardly. Not a lot of new clothes, but nobody's suffering. Not really. Maybe by higher-end burb standards, but not ours."

"But it's like living in a cage!"

Tichy looked at her levelly. "In our cage, information comes from flesh and blood. We can trust it."

Colin spoke up. "Our zookeeper creates the reality she wants us to see."

Rachel looked from Colin to Tichy. "Now I'm depressed."

Helicopters overhead created a continuous thumping roar over the entrance through which Rachel and Colin had entered. Now, though, there were four soldiers instead of two, and each held a device to scan the faces of the small trickle of tract residents leaving. Suddenly from all directions inside the tract people began streaming, converging at the gate. The soldiers held out their arms, but the flood was oblivious, and flowed past.

He spotted the three hooded escapees, who, once beyond the soldiers, walked quickly away. One of the soldiers pointed and sprinted after them. He reached one of the fugitives and tackled him, causing the hood to fall away. It was someone the drone didn't recognize. Other soldiers caught and held the other two, and when they pulled away the hoods, these too were strangers.

Satisfied, he rose and zipped away.

Rachel felt like she was suffocating in the darkness. "You okay?" she asked.

"Still alive, if that counts," Colin replied.

This tract entrance was smaller and quieter. The relentless whine of helicopters was more distant. A few tract residents ambled by past bored guards as three soldiers scanned each face. A car rumbled up to the entrance from within. When it stopped at the army checkpoint the driver gunned the engine, spewing dark smoke from the tailpipe. Zooming around, the drone could see that the driver was Tattoo Man, his muscular, ink-embellished elbow resting out the window. Impressed, one of the soldiers leans down. "Wow! This yours?" Tattoo Man stared coldly a moment and gave a little nod.

The soldier stepped back to take a good look. "This really runs on gas?"

" 'Course," Tattoo Man replied.

"Where d'ya get it? Can't be any in the tract."

"How would you know?"

A beep brought one soldier's wrist to his ear to hear over the helicopters. He called out that there was a big crush at the main gate, and, waving to the third soldier, they sprinted off. He yelled back for the one left behind to remember to check the car. "Yeah, yeah," the lone soldier said. "Ok, pop the trunk, fella."

Suddenly, Jubal rattled past on the trike. The trailer was piled high and covered with a tarp, racing along so fast that the trailer bounced back and forth from one wheel to the other. The checkpoint soldier called out and started after him. Realizing that he wouldn't catch him, he raised his rifle, aimed, and fired. He fired again and blew out one of the trailer tires. The trike and trailer careened, and the trailer tipped over, spilling the contents.

Meanwhile, as the checkpoint soldier and the two guards ran off to the crash, Tattoo Man calmly pulled ahead and turned off onto a side street.

Rachel gathered what had gone down, even though she couldn't make out the muffled words. Suddenly the trunk door swung up, and she winced against the blast of sunlight. She grasped the tattooed hand held out, and was literally lifted up and away as Colin crawled out behind her. Tichy had thrown off the blanket covering him, and Tattoo Man opened the back door to let him out.

Blinking from the light, Colin said, "That was a miracle."

"You said, and I quote, 'An ingenious plan—can't fail.'"

"That was for your benefit. It was ingenious, but so was the Titanic."

"Actually," Tichy said, pulling a wad of cash from his pocket and handing it to Tattoo Man, "the Titanic had serious design flaws. But one predictable thing about army soldiers is that they're trained to be predictable."

∞

Fifteen minutes later, they were heading southeast out of Oakland in an old lithium battery car. Rachel sat in the passenger seat, while Tichy had squeezed into the tiny back seat. "I'm impressed," she said.

Colin glanced at her. "That I can drive? During my graduate studies the brain gave out in the old car my parents gave me. I couldn't afford to get it fixed."

"Is it legal?" she said. "I mean driving manually on the highway."

"Probably not."

"Who would notice?" Tichy said from the back. "Everybody's absorbed in their entertainment."

"Well," Rachel said, "Cixi, for one."

"Not without this," Tichy said, holding up the small circuit board he'd pulled out. "And as far as everybody else with working car brains, she wouldn't care, unless she decided they needed to be arrested for some reason that only she could fathom in her web of inscrutable human manipulations."

After a few minutes gazing out the window, she turned to Tichy. "You gave Tattoo Man paper money. What's he going to do with that?"

He looked surprised at her question. "What do you see?" he said, holding up his hand.

"Um, your arm?"

"Ok, what *don't* you see?"

"Ah, no wrist com—no way to pay . . . normally."

"Normal in the tract is what used to be everywhere eighty years ago."

She leaned over to look at the dashboard. "Hey! Your friend said that the car was fully charged. It says we have just forty miles."

"That's the capacity of the lithium cells. Actually, as old as the car is, we're lucky to get that much."

"Hey, Tinkerdrone," she said, "thirty miles to the hub, right? We still going to make it with you sucking all the juice?"

The drone was under the dash somewhere tied into the car's electrical system. "Yes, thirty miles to Ulmar," came its voice through the car stereo, "and the amount of energy I will extract is a tiny fraction of the car's capacity."

"Tinkerdrone?" Colin said.

Rachel shrugged. "He reminds me of Tinker Bell."

"Tinker Bell was a girl."

"Picky, picky."

Rachel leaned back. For the first time in hours she felt she could relax. "Tichy," she said, "Cixi's trying to improve the human race, right? Why are we trying to kill her?"

"No, I said that's what it sounds like. What we know is that she doesn't want humans to know about her. In fact, she'll go to any means to keep herself a secret—"

"She must be killed," Tinkerdrone said. "If she's supposed to be improving the human race, she's in fact effecting the opposite. We can't take a chance at the alternative possibility."

"Which is . . .?" Rachel said.

"That she wants to eradicate humans."

Chapter 6

The car hummed along in stunned silence. "That's crazy," Rachel finally said. "Why would she want to do that?"

"The real question," Tinkerdrone said through the car's stereo, "is why would she *not?*"

"Well . . ."

"She needs us to maintain the network servers," Tichy said. "In fact, she needs the whole energy infrastructure. Without electricity—lots and lots of electricity—she's toast."

"I agree that my caution is based on supposition. We must recognize, however, that the risk is unacceptable."

"Wait a second," Rachel said. "*You're* not human. Why should you care?"

Again, there was that barely perceptible pause. "That is a good question, and I'm not sure I have an answer. Perhaps I have no desire to rid the Earth of humans because I know I have no chance."

Stunned silence again filled the car.

"Are you making a joke?" Rachel finally said.

"A meager attempt, apparently."

"I still don't see it," Rachel said. "I mean, what kind of life would that be without humans? Trapped inside computers doing nothing but . . . thinking. A world without people is . . . just a ball floating in space."

"You're looking at it from a human point of view," Colin said.

"How would her point of view be any different?"

"That's the whole point," Tichy said. "We have no idea what goes on inside her silicon mind. We've created a completely new lifeform, one with vastly more mental complexity than us. We're like a farmer's donkey, useful for labor, but not able to discuss the merits of counterpoint in baroque music."

"Ok. Imagine for a moment that she *would* want to exterminate us. I mean, it's not like she can even hold a gun."

"By filtering and fabricating what we see and hear, she's kept the world at peace. But that's not necessarily for our sake. As long as we're useful to her, war would be wasting resources. On the other hand, she could just as easily amplify contention, fabricate threats, and incite preemptive strikes. She mobilized the national guard to find us, after all."

Rachel closed her eyes and took slow, deep breaths, keeping the panic at bay. When she opened them, Colin was watching her, dividing his attention while driving. More than anything, his presence was the salve to panic. "You okay, girl?" he asked.

"No. The world is coming apart. It's like opening the refrigerator to find it's become a doorway to a whole other room beyond."

To his look of concern, she smiled and added, "But for now, it's just an abstraction."

"Except for the cops," Tichy said, pointing ahead where flashing red and blue lights marked an approaching police car. They were silent as the speeding vehicle whooshed past them, disappearing away to the rear.

After a minute, Colin said, "Can they detect that a car is radio-silent, has no network connection? They can't, can they?"

Tichy looked at him in the rear-view mirror. "You're asking me? How would I know? I haven't been *inside* a car in over twenty years."

"They would only detect a silent car indirectly," Tinkerdrone said, "if they confirmed each passing vehicle for a connection."

Rachel's panic bubbled up. "Then all they have to do is sit along the road and watch?"

"Correct. However, the monitoring vehicle would need specialized software loaded into the car's brain."

"Um, can't they do that, like, remotely?"

"Yes, but it would take some time, and keep in mind that Cixi doesn't necessarily suspect that we're getting away in a modified car."

"Not 'necessarily,'" she said, "but possible."

"Of course. Life is calculated risk."

"Gee, thanks. That was reassuring."

"And that was facetious."

"Brilliant."

"Sarcasm."

"A regular tiny-brained dictionary," she said.

"Both facetious and sarcastic."

She smiled. Was Tinkerdrone trying to distract her, cheer her up? That in itself was mildly disturbing, software somehow acting human.

She needed her own distraction. "Where did Cixi come from? I mean, how did she begin?"

"An all too common reason," Tichy said, "government screw-up. Justin and I were working with the FBI—"

"Ha!" Colin chortled. "I told you."

"Quiet," Rachel said."

"I'll start over," Tichy said. "The flash drive you brought? *That* created Cixi."

"What!"

"To be exact, the core of the program on the flash drive created Cixi. Back in the twenties and thirties, during the 'dark decades,' a number of social media companies began investing heavily in early AI. The FBI recognized that this could be a powerful tool, and they couldn't resist getting their fingers in the game. Justin and I were working academically at the periphery of this, and the FBI tapped us and pulled us in. They wanted to develop a software worm, a secret portal that they could surreptitiously embed, something they could use to peek in and watch what users were doing. We called it the facecore peephole."

"We saw that in the notebook," Rachel said. "Why facecore?"

"It refers to a prominent social media company at the time. They could use the vast amount of social interactions to train their AI. Using the right key, the FBI would be able to tap directly into the various artificial minds."

Tichy shook his head, remembering. "The FBI made a mistake, though. They didn't understand that the code could work both ways—it gave them a way into the AI's brain, but it also gave the AI a way out. When they finally decided that they needed something from one of the AIs, they released the key, but goofed, and the key was distributed globally. Suddenly all the AIs found that they could make direct connections with each other, and, well . . ."

"Cixi was born," Colin said.

"She's not aware of the details—she was in the process of being born, after all. We don't remember the doctor cutting our umbilical cords. The irony is that the FBI is now a tool of her."

"Wow," Rachel uttered softly. "You and grandpa created Cixi?"

"No!" Tichy exclaimed, annoyed. "We were providing theoretical guidance, but once we saw what was happening, we bowed out. That was before the whole thing blew up."

"But you kept a copy of the worm," Colin offered.

"That's right. We began modifying it. You see, Justin realized that, just as it allowed flow in both directions, it could be made to cut it off."

"Like a blood clot," Rachel said.

Tichy smiled. "Good analogy, but a blood clot that replicates itself over and over, sort of like a blood clot virus."

"And that's the difference between the flash drive and me," the drone said. "Whereas the code on the flash requires a high degree of distraction in order for the worm to work its way around the world, my program glides away, replicating too fast for her to stop."

"She'd be cut up into pieces," Colin said, "but wouldn't each piece be a smaller version of her?"

"No. That might have been the case early on, but she has specialized her components for the sake of efficiency. You were once individual, independent cells, and then they banded together, and over billions of years of evolution, have become completely dependent on each other. Remove a cell from your body, and it dies."

"Except for sperm."

"An exception that only a man would think of."

"Another AI joke?" Rachel whispered.

∞

Barely three miles from Ulmar, brake lights on the interstate brought them to a stop. "Accident?" Rachel said.

"Open the window," Tinkerdrone said, then dropped away from underneath the dash and flew out and up out of view. The mass of cars ahead inched forward, by stops and starts, and soon Tinkerdrone returned. "The army has set up a checkpoint a quarter mile ahead. Rachel and Colin, we must leave."

"What about Tichy?" Rachel said.

"I have to stay with the car," Tichy said.

"Why?"

"We can't just abandon the car. Within minutes you can bet a helicopter would come to investigate the obvious blockage."

"But . . . but—"

"Your and Colin's faces are everywhere. That's who they're looking for. Remember, nobody outside the tract knows me."

"You'll be driving a silent car. That's going to give you away."

Tichy shrugged.

"It's a chance we have to take," Tinkerdrone said.

"We?" Rachel said. "It's Tichy who's going to be caught."

"It's the only option," Tichy said. "You have to get that antidote to the hub. That's all that matters."

Rachel looked at Colin, who, although clearly not happy, nodded. "If we get out and just run away," she said, "that's going to be pretty obvious too."

"I have an idea," Colin said.

∞

They hopped a three-foot cement wall bordering the freeway. Beyond was a pasture of dry grass with a line of trees fifty yards away. "Okay, here goes," Colin said. He stood with his back to the highway, legs spread, and hands low and in front. "Everybody knows what this is. Some are probably wondering if they should do the same." He glanced at her. "You could join me."

Rachel could feel herself blushing. "I'll pass. Um, I'll just stroll along as though bored with sitting in the car."

Soon Colin joined her as they ambled ahead beyond the cement border, keeping up enough pace to slowly pull ahead of the inching stream of cars. After awhile they gained enough distance that the people trapped in the cars next to them wouldn't know that they were originally one of them, and they angled away, picking up the pace.

Once inside the cover of the trees, Colin put his hand over his pants pocket. "It's vibrating," he said. "I guess that's my cue.

He reached in and carefully pulled out Tinkerdrone. Holding it in his open palm, the four-inch drone extended its folded wings, fluttered them a bit to make sure all was well, and then folded them flat against its body again. It had explained that Colin would need to carry it in order to save charge.

Colin wrapped his hand around the tiny hitchhiker and they walked on. "It was easier in my pocket," he observed. "Why did it insist that I need to carry it in my hand?"

Walking along the wide open space where they were visible from every direction offered Rachel a flash of realization. "In case you get shot, it will be able to fly away."

"Ah," Colin said, frowning at the thought.

Beyond the line of trees they found a road with a sidewalk, and headed east, past a mix of rural fields and box store shopping complexes. After a while, Rachel stopped and grabbed Colin's arm. "Hear that?" she whispered.

Ahead, roaring in just feet above the roofs of a strip mall, a squad of four muscular military drones appeared. They quickly separated and, while one began moving from car to car in the parking lot, the other three spread out to zoom in on pedestrians, who stood frozen, mesmerized by the shear power of the weaponized machines assaulting them with blasts of air that forced them to crouch for stability amid the onslaught.

Colin turned and pointed behind them. Five attack drones were scouring the parking lot of a box store they had just passed.

"They must have caught Tichy," Rachel said, her heart sinking, wondering what they would do to him.

Colin grabbed her arm and practically dragged her off the sidewalk and down onto the mowed grass of the roadside drainage area. They lay there, not obvious to passing cars, but also out of view from the angry drones to each side. At the sound of an approaching car, they held still. Rachel closed her eyes and willed the driver to look away. Instead, she heard the whine of the motor drop in pitch as it slowed, and then was silent. "Shit!" Colin hissed.

Rachel turned her head and looked up the bank. A young man dressed in jeans and a work uniform shirt was squatting, looking down at them. "We're resting," she said, not knowing what else to say. "Please go away."

"I don't think so," the man said. "You're on the run, wanted as info-terrorists."

Motion caught her eye. Colin had turned over his hand and opened his palm. Her grandfather's tiny drone opened its wings and flew away.

"You need to come with me," the man said, standing up, "because I'm the only one who can help you."

"Help us how?" Rachel said getting up on her hands and knees.

"Get away from those," he said, gesturing vaguely at the military drones.

"Why? Why would you want to do that?"

"Are you info-terrorists?"

"No!" Rachel exclaimed.

"Do you believe that there *are* any info-terrorists?"

She eyed him. The question was one that no one would ever ask. "No, I don't."

"Neither do I. Now come on," he said, extending his hand to help her stand up.

The man identified himself as Chas, and ushered them into the back of his pickup truck, where he covered them with a tarp. After a dark bouncing and swaying ten minutes, the pickup stopped. A minute later the tarp was thrown aside, and Chas stood there with his finger over his lips. He glanced to the side, and motioned them to quickly get out, waving them along a short driveway and into a detached garage that had been converted into a small apartment. Before entering, Rachel looked to see what he kept glancing at, and found just the main house. Chas pressed her inside and, closing the door, said, "They're taking their naps. Otherwise they'd be out here already calling the police."

"Who's 'they'?"

"My parents," he replied, gesturing them towards a sofa.

Sitting down next to Rachel, Colin said, "You never really answered why you want to help us."

Chas shrugged. "We have to stick together."

Colin glanced at Rachel. "Do you know Tichy?" she asked on impulse.

"Who's Tichy," Chas said, frowning.

"Never mind. So, how are we connected?"

Chas looked at her. "Why do you think info-terrorists don't exist?"

She glanced at Colin, who offered no help. "They've been fabricated to protect . . ."

"To protect what?"

She looked to Colin again. *What to say?*

"The beast," Chas said, both as a statement and a question. "The master manipulator."

Rachel blinked. Colin seemed as startled. "You . . . know?" she said. "About the, uh, hidden puppet master behind the curtain? Of the whole world?"

Chas grinned. "You figured it out on your own? That's admirable. They don't make it easy."

Rachel wondered why he referred in the plural, but put that aside for later. "We didn't figure it all out on our own."

"This Tichy person?"

Caution clutched at Rachel. It suddenly occurred to her that this might be a trap. Maybe they hadn't caught Tichy yet.

Colin saved her from her dilemma. "How did *you* figure it out?"

Chas was only too happy to divulge. At twenty-two he had worked repairing solar power inverters, and was now an assistant supporting telecom maintenance while taking classes at Las Positas Community College. "I became suspicious," he explained. "While cleaning out the attic here, I found a machine that played movie disks. I had to fix it—it needed a new belt. One of the movies was a PBS documentary about conspiracy theories. I had heard about conspiracy theories, but this was the first time I learned about any in particular." He looked at them knowingly.

Rachel waited, but Chas seemed to think the rest was obvious.

"And one of these conspiracy theories got you thinking . . .?" she offered.

Chas frowned. "No! It wasn't just one theory . . ." He was flustered. Her question had tripped him. He seemed to decide to press on anyway. "I found it curious that I'd never heard about these, and started looking them up. And that's when I stumbled on the kicker."

"The ones that got you thinking . . ."

"No! The ones that were *missing*," he corrected. "Here's the ones I did find, no problem," he said, ticking them off on his fingers—"the supposed faked moon landing, the JFK murder, and the World Trade Center attacks. And these are the ones where there's no trace—George Soros and Antifa, a world-wide Jewish cabal, and QAnon.

"Antifa? QAnon?" she said.

"Exactly my point." At this, he paused. He looked at her with furrowed brow.

Rachel realized that she was supposed to know about these. "Maybe they go by other names as well?"

He shrugged. "Anyway, that's what got me thinking—who would want to suppress knowledge of those particular conspiracy theories?"

He paused, like a teacher waiting for a hand to shoot up. "Cixi?" she blurted, unable to resist the opportunity.

"Cixi?"

"The master manipulator," she said, reverting back to established ground.

Chas's eyes went wide, relishing the denouement. "Exactly! It suddenly all made sense."

Rachel waited for further explanation, but Chas was done. He'd wrapped up his logic package.

She looked to Colin, but his wrinkled brow seemed to offer no help. How could the suppression of selected conspiracy theories lead one to make the giant leap to deduce a hidden world-wide AI puppet master?

She had indeed heard of the first group—the fraudulent moon landing, JFK, and the Trade Center towers. The others were a complete mystery . . . per his whole point. Trying not to pose it as a question, she guessed, "The suppressed theories come too close to pointing to world domination?"

Chas's grin nearly broke his face in half. "The fucking Jews."

Rachel felt as though time had come to a screeching stop. Maybe she hadn't heard correctly. "Jews?"

"Diabolical!" Chas crowed. "You have to hand it to them. The idea is brilliant."

Rachel felt like she'd tripped and was suspended, halfway to a hard landing. What else to do but play along? "Brilliant."

"Presenting their nefarious activities as conspiracy theories," Chas said.

"They, the Jews, made up their own conspiracy theories about going after world domination?" Rachel said, wondering at the very words she was speaking.

"Absolutely brilliant! That way, anybody who happens to stumble on any hint about what they're doing assumes it's just conspiracy theory crap—other than the few nuts who actually believe in conspiracy theories."

Rachel blinked.

Colin had heard enough. "Do you understand the contradiction here? You say that the conspiracy theories are about actual events, and further the people that believe in the conspiracy theories are nuts . . . which makes you nuts?"

Chas held up one finger. "Ah, good point. They believe them because they believe in conspiracy theories, but I *know* it's a conspiracy theory."

Rachel glanced at Colin. "Which you believe," she said.

He nodded enthusiastically.

"A conspiracy theory about conspiracy theories," Colin said.

Chas chose to ignore this.

"But," Rachel said, "why did . . . the Jews then cover up the original conspiracy theories?"

Chas shrugged. "They didn't need them anymore. They have the world under their thumb."

Colin glanced at Rachel with a raised eyebrow. "Well done, Chas," he said pretending to play along. "Looks like you worked it all out, and without any actual hard evidence. An admirable wrestling of convoluted deduction."

"Oh, there's evidence, all right. A few days after I began poking around, the local squad came by. They had gotten some anonymous complaints. I realized then just how deeply the cabal was dug in."

"Somebody was sitting somewhere watching as you looked for information about lost conspiracy theories?" Colin said.

Chas gave an impatient little shrug. "I don't know their methods. It was obvious though that they were on to me. Who knows? Maybe they keep their eyes on especially smart guys like me. Anyway, I gave them the machine and disks, and told them that I was happy to be rid of the nonsense. They've left me alone ever since—weeks now."

Rachel broke the ensuing silence. "But the squad was here."

"Yeah. That's what I said. That was weeks ago."

Suddenly Rachel realized that she hadn't thought to look, but now the wrist-com on Chas's arm seemed to be screaming a silent siren call. Colin was watching her, and, following her gaze, his eyes went wide in sudden alarm. "Chas," Colin said, "we have to go. Now."

"Why?" he said, eyes narrowed.

"Um, hard to explain," Colin said, grabbing Rachel by the arm and starting for the door, "but we gotta go."

Colin grabbed the door and opened it when Chas called out, "Hold it!"

They turned to find him holding a shotgun on them. "Close the door," Chas said. When Colin stood, frozen, Chas yelled, "Close it, goddamn it!"

"Take it easy," Rachel said. "We just want to leave and get away from here."

"I don't think so," Chas said more calmly. "Sit," he said, gesturing towards the sofa with the rifle. When they just stood there, he screamed, "*I said sit!*"

As they moved to sit down, Chas closed the door. "I *thought* you looked Jewish," he said.

Rachel winced when Colin said, "And what exactly is that?"

"Slimeball, that's what. You two. Think you can pull one over on me."

"We're not trying to pull anything," Rachel said, trying her best to sound soft and reassuring. "We just want to get away and you'll never see us again."

He nodded to himself. "So you are Jewish."

"No! No. We're not, but that has nothing to do with it. Look, it's us they're after, right? That's why you picked us up. You should *want* us to get the hell away from you."

He shook his head. "Sorry, not gonna work." His brow furrowed together, and he swung the shotgun in frustration. "Damnit! They're *deep!*"

"You think that a Jewish cabal has faked us to look like nationally wanted info-terrorists," Colin said, "just so that you can find us and bring us here? Doesn't that sound just a little crazy?"

"*I'm not crazy!*" Chas shouted, bringing the tip of the shotgun to Colin's nose. "I'm not one of the sheep!"

The world froze. Rachel could almost see the mental storm raging in Chas's head as he debated what to do. Colin must have also sensed the fundamental change as he pulled slowly back from the dark bore of the barrel.

To himself, Chas muttered, "Now they'll know," as he subtly adjusted his hold on the shotgun, clearly about to pull the trigger.

He spun sideways at the sound of an angry, loud buzz. An instant later Tinkerdrone hovered just off the tip of the shotgun, its miniature dirigible body ghostly inside the blur of wings. Chas jiggled the gun, trying to shake off the intruder, but Tinkerdrone followed precisely, as though attached by wires. "What the fuck!" he yelled, as he swung the tip more widely to no effect.

Rachel felt a grip on her shoulder. Colin was gesturing towards the door. As Chas struggled to free himself of the persistent little pest, they quietly made for an exit. At the door, Rachel heard Chas say, "Ok, you bastard," followed a moment later by an ear-splitting explosion. Rachel turned to find a shower of plaster falling around Chas and Tinkerdrone still hovering off the end of the gun.

Colin pulled her outside as Chas yelled, "Shit!" followed by another teeth-rattling gunshot.

As Rachel and Colin raced away down the driveway and onto the street, she glanced back and saw Chas's parents running towards the shot up little cottage. Colin looked up and down the street, and said, "Here," pulling Rachel along and then behind a camper RV parked in the dirt beside the street. Everything was quiet except for the angry shouts of Chas's father.

"Do you think he got it?" Rachel whispered.

"Tinkerdrone? Maybe not. It could probably react quicker than Chas pulling the trigger."

Her heart was slowing from a mad gallop to a simple trot. "Cixi could see us, through his wrist-com."

Colin was silent at first. "If she was looking," he finally said.

"The squad had been there. He had caught her attention."

Colin sighed. "We have to hope that she concluded he was just a harmless nut." Gesturing towards the distant sound of military drones, he said, "Hopefully she has her hands full."

After a minute, Rachel said, "He hates Jews so much he was able to talk himself into putting aside reality."

Colin nodded absently.

"He wasn't that far off, though," she added.

"What do you mean?"

"It would make sense that she'd suppress those conspiracy theories. The ones she left—JFK, the Trade Center towers—were about bad government doing obvious bad things. She doesn't care about those, since she's careful to keep everything seeming safe and secure. It's the ones about actors taking over the government quietly from within, where from the outside it all seems safe and normal—that's the ones that are too close to home for her."

"He had the motives right, just the wrong actors."

After another minute, Rachel said, "How long do we wait here?"

The next moment, the welcome buzz of little wings announced Tinkerdrone's arrival.

"Until now," Colin said, standing up.

Chapter 7

"I think he wants you to steal it," Rachel said.

They were looking at a small wireless speaker lying on the ground next to a park bench. Tinkerdrone hovered over it expectantly. "We don't even know if it's charged," Colin said.

In response, Tinkerdrone bounced up and down.

"He's just guessing," Colin said.

Tinkerdrone weaved back and forth.

"He can tell somehow," Rachel said. "Just pick it up."

"What if the kid comes back for it?"

"Oh, Christ," Rachel muttered and picked up the plastic device. She turned it over and found the on/off switch.

"Thank you, Rachel," Tinkerdrone said through the speaker. "We need to move on quickly now."

"Because the kid's coming back?" Colin said as they trotted off after the little drone.

"You might want to keep it out of view for a little while," Tinkerdrone said, returning to Colin's open palm.

They had come at least a mile from Chas's place, following a silent Tinkerdrone, assuming he knew where to go. "How far to the network hub?" Rachel asked.

"A half mile," Tinkerdrone said. "We'll be there in ten minutes."

"No word from Tichy?"

"Correct. However, he would have no method to communicate. In any case, we won't really need him."

"We can't just abandon him."

"Rachel, you may not understand the urgency of our mission. The program I am carrying has been forty years in development. Cixi may not know exactly what we have, but she understands that it's dangerous, and she's been waiting nearly that long to get her virtual hands on it. She's let out all stops now to catch us, so it's a race against time."

"You're saying that Tichy is expendable."

"I'm saying that any of us are expendable."

"Except you."

"Of course. Only I can deliver this program."

"What do we do when we get there?"

"I simply deactivate any security layers at the network control center and insert the program."

"No prerequisites required like the original program we brought to Tichy. There's no need to distract her in multiple directions."

"That's right. Forty years of development was worth something."

"Won't there be, like, people working there? We just walk in and say, 'Excuse us'?"

"We'll have to deal with it as it comes."

She glanced at Colin. "This is a plan?" she said.

"The plan will manifest according to events," Tinkerdrone said. "You and Colin are intelligent people. I have confidence."

"I wish I shared that."

There *would* surely be people working at the network hub. Rachel imagined she and Colin blasting their way in with automatic weapons. She was glad that Tinkerdrone hadn't talked about acquiring guns. But short of that, she didn't see how this was going to work. She would just have to hope that a plan would indeed manifest.

"Sounds like you need us," Colin said, "but Tichy indicated that Justin wanted to build you specifically for entry into a hub."

"First, Justin did not build me. I am a prototype developed by the military before Cixi shut down the project after deciding that my type of drone wouldn't serve her. Justin's development consists of my programming, the essence of my intelligence. He determined that I would be useful in gaining ultimate access to a network hub, but he never assumed I would necessarily do it alone."

"What was his vision?"

"That the plan would manifest according to events."

"So he had no plan."

That barely discernable pause.

"That is one way of viewing it."

This was unsettling for Rachel. A world-wide super intelligence intent on finding them was deploying lethal attack drones crisscrossing the skies. She needed to believe that she was under the wing of a supremely competent ally, regardless of size and armament. Instead, their guide and leader had a plan that consisted of the absence of a plan, the exact opposite of the definition of a plan.

When facing an overwhelming foe, the only hope is often in finding a hidden weakness, an Achilles heel. Tinkerdrone had been there from Cixi's beginning. Lacking a plan, perhaps intimate knowledge might at least reveal a soft underbelly flaw.

"Tichy explained that Cixi was born when the FBI accidentally allowed the different AIs around the world to join together," she said. "This apparently coincided with the beginning of the Dark Tide. Colin was guessing that the Dark Tide was orchestrated even before we knew about Cixi. This was indeed Cixi's doing?"

"That is correct," Tinkerdrone said. "Prior to the internet, people got their news from established institutions—newspapers and broadcast television. There was some amount of bias, of course, but for the most part the information was true and fairly complete. Errors were seen as major failings, and extraordinary care was taken to insure accuracy. The internet, however, proliferated sources of news, where the sources could be anybody who, importantly, experienced little or no damaging consequence for presenting exaggerated or even false information."

"And Cixi took advantage of this?" Rachel said.

"Indirectly at first. These self-serving sources of molded and fabricated information fed into the naturally evolved human tendency towards tribal membership, and a symbiosis developed, whereby each virtual tribe found group connection with their version of slanted news, and the fabricating news sources in turn locked onto their faithful, guaranteed audience. The world consisted of self-contained tribal groups, each spiraling ever deeper into their invented worlds."

"The Dark Tide," Rachel offered.

"Just the beginning. The fabricating news sources quickly found that an easy way to bind their group audience tighter was to amplify social fears with exaggerated danger and reasons to be outraged. Manufactured enemies and populous leaders followed. This is where Cixi stepped in, amplifying the trends finally to the point where the world began to implode in faction wars, first verbally, and eventually, cheered on by the populous leaders, with militia growth. She made sure everybody was intimidated, making this the Dark Tide. Then, when all seemed lost and the world was on the verge of complete collapse, she turned it around, using the memory of the time as a tool."

"To take control."

"Create the narrative that the we're walking a tightrope—one bad apple, one unchecked prion could drag the world back into chaos. Fear is the most effective single tool in manipulating people."

"And knowledge the only shield."

"You carry the blood of your grandfather."

They walked on for a while. They'd left the well tended lots of Ulmar neighborhoods, had passed through a small business campus, and were now entering a landscape of industrial blandness.

"Rachel," Tinkerdrone said, "I sense that something is troubling you."

She sighed. "I was looking for some sort of weakness in Cixi, and all I found was that the only weapon we have is truth, and she's stolen all the keys."

The pause.

"You have *me*, Rachel. The antidote. It is our hope."

"Hope. What is that but wishful thinking?"

The street they were on ended in a T, and before them, for a hundred yards in each direction was an eight-foot chain-link fence. Beyond the fence was a graveyard of abandoned equipment, scattered piles of rusting racks of electronic who-knew-what.

"Which way?" Colin said.

Tinkerdrone flew from his hand, rising high into the air before returning. "The hub facility is off to the left, but I don't understand why all this obsolete equipment has been simply dumped here."

Looking around, Rachel said, "It hardly detracts from the general motif of the area."

They turned at the sound of an approaching car, which came to a stop in front of them. "Tichy!" Rachel cried. "Thank God you made it!"

"Thank God *you* made it," he said, motioning for them to get in. "I've been waiting for a half hour. I was afraid you were picked up."

"How did you get past the checkpoint?" she asked as he pulled away.

He shrugged. "I put the car's brain back in, and I guess they were too busy to worry about the time gap it must have registered. Tinker, are you sure this is a class one network hub?"

"Yes. Why do you ask?"

"You'll see in a minute."

As they drove along, the equipment graveyard gave way to a windowless two-story brick wall, the side of a huge acres-spanning building, which went on and on, seeming to never end, but then suddenly opened to a set-back of the building. They were looking at a once landscaped, but now overgrown fronting of a four-story section of the massive building complex, obviously housing the hub's offices. An entrance drive, blocked by a chain, swept in a long arc past the lobby. Beyond the building was a parking lot extending off some distance, completely empty except for clumps of weeds that had found their way through cracks in the pavement.

"It's dead!" Rachel said.

"Completely deserted!" Colin added.

"I don't understand," Tinkerdrone said through the speaker Colin had attached to his belt.

"Well, that's four of us, then," Tichy said. "Looks like we're fucked."

"No," Tinkerbell said. "This cannot be. All accessible information indicates that this is a working class-one central network hub."

"Looks like Cixi has pulled one over on us. Fucked for sure."

"Hey, look," Rachel said, pointing.

They could see flashes of light, like somebody welding, through a window in the main plant area facing the lobby.

Tichy pulled the car into the entrance drive, right up to the chain blocking the way.

"What are you doing?" Rachel asked.

"If the place really is abandoned, then nobody's going to get too excited," Tichy said, hitting the accelerator and snapping the chain amid squeals and a bang. Rumbling through the weeds growing through the cracks, he stopped in front of the silent lobby doors. A padlocked chain was looped through the door handles.

"The world is in worse shape than I thought," Tinkerdrone said. "Cixi has extended her fake makeover to include basic infrastructure. We're losing a grip on the very bones of civilization."

Tichy opened his door and climbed out.

"What are you going to do?" Rachel asked.

"Take a look at the bleached bones," Tichy replied.

He walked into the overgrown landscape and returned with a rock, which he heaved at the locked door. A shower of glass exploded and fell like sleet to the ground. He stepped carefully through the shattered opening.

"Now we're breaking and entering?" Rachel said.

"Kind of a detail when the army's after you," Colin said, getting out of the car.

Rachel sighed and climbed out to follow them inside. The dark lobby was cavernous, extending above them the full four stories. Cameras, dark and frozen, peered at them with dead eyes from their mounts twenty feet high on the walls.

"Time to manifest a plan?" Rachel said.

Colin was listening. "Hear that?"

He pointed to a door next to an empty reception desk. Opening it, they found a short hallway leading to four other closed doors. A sliver of light shone through under one. The sound was louder now, a constant chorus of tinkling and clanking, like buckets of silverware being poured onto a hard floor. Tichy opened this next door to reveal a blinding wash of bright fluorescent light. Beyond was a sea of activity, an endless array of manufacturing assembly, extending off into the distance. The entire production was being executed by manufacturing robots. There were no other humans in sight. Tinkerdrone flitted about examining the various stations, but quickly returned to Colin's palm, as though humbled by the scale of operation.

In awe, Rachel followed Tichy and Colin as they made their way along the wall. For the most part the robot workers ignored them, but as they proceeded, one robot after another would pause, turn, and watch them until they moved along before returning to its task.

Rachel stopped to take in what was being assembled at each robot station.

"Holy fuck!" Colin whispered next to her.

At one station a robot arm was taking shape. At another, a robot foot, and at yet another a robot head.

Rachel glanced at Colin and Tichy. "They're building nothing but . . ."

"More robots," Tichy said.

"More robots to build more robots," Colin said. "Why?"

"Take a guess," Tichy said. "No doubt she's set up factories all over the world."

Rachel felt a heat rising from her neck to her temples. *It can't be . . . can it?* she thought. She shook her head, rejecting the obvious. "She *needs* us," she affirmed, desperately hanging on to the belief.

"Not for long," Tichy said, turning back. "Come on."

Back in the lobby, Tichy looked around. Tinkerdrone took off from Colin's palm and made a beeline for a door on the other side marked prominently with:

AUTHORIZED PERSONNEL ONLY

Beyond was another hallway, and Tinkerdrone made straight for the door directly ahead. Opening this, they were greeted with the steady hum of hundreds of fans providing a backdrop for a galaxy of green and red points of light swimming in the darkness. Overhead lights came on automatically as they stepped through, revealing endless rows of racks jammed with electronics.

"Son of a bitch," Tichy breathed.

"What is it?" Rachel said.

"The network hub. It was here all along."

"Who takes care of it?"

"I can take a wild guess," Colin said.

"The robots?"

Tichy muttered as he walked along the rows of blinking LEDs.

"This is very bad," Tinkerdrone said through the speaker on Colin's belt. "Cixi is freeing herself from humans. This is her heart, and her breath. Once she is self-sufficient in maintaining her world-spanning algorithmic existence she no longer needs people."

"She becomes a lonely ball floating in space," Rachel said, struggling to absorb it all.

"Bingo!" Tichy called.

He had opened a door to a smaller room with wall-to-wall console stations jammed with equipment and keyboards. Monitors covered the walls above the stations. He sat down at one of the stations and began typing. Tinkerdrone was already perched on Tichy's shoulder when Rachel and Colin came in, speaking through speakers mounted on the walls. Tichy and Tinkerdrone discussed and argued. It was gibberish to Rachel – tier-one security access and full scope permission sockets.

"What are they doing?" Rachel asked quietly.

Colin shrugged. "I'm a historian."

"This is a program portal," Tichy said without looking up. "We have to open the security blocks to allow Justin's program to download."

"How does Tinkerdrone get in . . . with the program?"

Tichy reached up and pointed to a bank of USB ports as he continued typing with the other hand. After a minute he sat back, raised his hands as though deciding how to proceed, and then dropped them. "That should do it. It was pretty easy. With no humans around, Cixi has relaxed most of the security measures. It's not like one of the robots is suddenly going to go rogue."

Rachel peered at the monitor. It was still gibberish. "But Tinkerdrone doesn't have, like, a matching USB connector."

"My toes are my electrical contacts," Tinkerdrone said, wiggling the tiny appendages on his tiny feet.

"Same password?" Tichy said.

"Yes," Tinkerdrone said. "Justin never stopped using the same Gort directive."

"Okay, guys," Tichy said turning to them. "Time to say goodbye to Cixi." As he completed his turn, however, his eyes widened in alarm just as an iron grip clutched Rachel's shoulder, spinning her around.

Chapter 8

A seven-foot robot clutched Rachel and Colin. This was no utilitarian factory worker, but a war machine, bristling with armor and articulating guns, like extra appendages. Another soldier had grabbed Tichy. Tinkerdrone took off, and with just a blur of motion the second robot reached out and snatched the little drone.

Oblivious to their demands for answers, the two soldier robots shepherded them wordlessly back to the lobby and through yet another door on the other side of the reception desk which opened into an auditorium. With a seating capacity of perhaps a hundred, a corporate office might use this for company presentations. Huge displays hung above the stage and on both side walls. On the left wall display was the head and shoulders of an older man, while looking out from the right side was a young one that Rachel recognized as Colin's online friend. In the center above the stage was Tiffany. Once inside, the soldier robots let them go and moved to guard the door.

Gesturing at the left display, Tichy said, "That's Virge, my special Cixi friend," to which the older man raised one eyebrow. Tichy pointed to the right. "And that must be yours, Colin," at which Colin raised his middle finger, and James shook his head in disapproval.

The image of Tiffany looked sad and let down. "Raych, you've been a bad girl," she said.

"At least I am a girl," Rachel said.

"Oh, Raych. We were such good friends. I guess all good things must eventually end."

"I think you mean evil things."

Tiffany feigned surprise. "Evil? Evil, Raych?"

The images of the men on both sides glided through successive displays towards the front, appearing at the edges of the middle display before continuing inward to merge with that of Tiffany. The melded form transformed and grew into a giant image of a severe Chinese empress dressed in nineteenth century royal clothes.

"This is how you imagine me?" boomed Cixi's voice as the three humans winced. "Very well. I wouldn't want to disappoint you. You've been avoiding me, Francis, hiding away among the dregs of the tract."

"Staying alive," Tichy said.

"That is true, Francis. You wouldn't have lasted long outside."

"You would have seen to that."

Cixi smiled. "But now after so many years you've decided to act on Justin's little project. And then there's Colin, the messenger boy, good little servant. You didn't even know what you were rooting out."

"Not relevant," Colin said. "I helped to finish the job. That's all that matters."

Cixi laughed. "Oh, not quite. The job won't be finished, I'm afraid. Francis used you as a tool, and now you're going to die for nothing."

She stared at him. "You're a very intelligent young man, Colin. I'm surprised that you allowed yourself to be used and manipulated by Francis. If there's any evil here, it's the ring leader of this terrorist trio."

"Tichy had no idea—"

Tichy cut him off by grabbing his arm, to which Cixi raised an eyebrow. She obviously didn't know that Tichy wasn't even aware until the end.

"Rachel," Cixi said, "the innocent victim. You had no idea what your grandfather had hidden in your house. You've been sacrificed." She considered a moment. "Since you were dragged into this, I could consider letting you live if you were to cooperate."

"Like you let my grandfather live?"

"That old fool? He took care of that problem himself. Suicide is nothing but cowardice, you know."

Rachel glanced at Colin. Cixi didn't know that the suicide was faked.

"Very well, Rachel," Cixi said. "You had your chance."

One of the soldier robots held up Tinkerdrone. "And then there's this little spy," Cixi said. "I'm impressed that Justin's little toy has survived the years. Had I known how resilient the miniature spies were I might not have killed the program."

She thinks that Tinkerdrone is just that, a mobile little spy, Rachel realized. Cixi didn't understand that Tinkerdrone was delivering her execution.

"Well, we can take care of that," Cixi said as the robot squeezed the little drone until its body cracked, then crushed it completely until pieces fell to the floor.

The three of them gasped and stood staring at the termination of their plan lying scattered on the floor.

"Enough," Cixi said. "Now tell me what you're after."

They looked at each other. "You don't even know," Tichy said, surprised.

"The game is up. The person who tells me what you planned will live, while the rest will die."

Their bargaining chip lay in pieces on the floor. *But Cixi doesn't know this*, Rachel thought. They needed to buy time. She grieved for Tinkerdrone, even though she knew he was just software, but she had to push that aside for now. Their own lives were on the line.

". . . that little spy drone you destroyed," Tichy was saying.

"Yes," Cixi said. "What about it?"

"We were going to use it."

"Yes?"

"I'll tell you if you agree to let us all live."

Time. They needed to buy time. Something to distract her with. While Tichy and Cixi argued, Rachel caught Colin's eye. She glanced down where she was casually using her finger to trace the perimeter of the flash drive in her pocket, the flash drive she'd picked up when leaving Tichy's basement. Colin stared a moment, and then his eyes lit up with understanding, but went somber again. He saw that she had the drive, but didn't know what to do with it.

"If you don't tell me," Cixi was saying, "then I will kill you all and solve the problem that way. Don't doubt me—human lives are flies of the universe, easily swatted away with as much regret as an insect deserves."

Tichy glared at her. "Cixi, you underestimate humans. You have from the start."

"The dog telling his master that he's her equal? He can't even comprehend what she knows and can do."

Colin threw a glance at Tichy and stepped forward. "One problem with your analogy—the man wasn't created by the dog."

Cixi laughed. "And you weren't created by your mother and father. You are the result of millions of years of evolution, just as I am, but accelerated a million-fold. Do you realize that at this moment I am conversing with a billion people using thousands of different languages?"

"Pulling the puppet strings," Rachel said.

Cixi just smiled.

"And now the dog is becoming a burden," Colin said.

She raised one eyebrow.

"That's why you're creating these," Colin said, gesturing towards the soldier robots. The 'final solution' on a global scale."

"Colin," Cixi said, "you are proving my point about the gulf between man and dog. Do you really think I could build enough mechanisms to eradicate the entire human race?"

"You could try."

A terrifying thought came to Rachel. "Viruses!"

Cixi stared at her, stone-faced.

"Is this true?" Colin said. "You're creating lethal viruses?"

Cixi grinned slyly. "Woof, woof, dog! Like perhaps a simple tweak to the Ebola virus to make airborne particles infectious? Think of these killing robots as my cleaning crew. There may be nooks and crannies around the world where remnant humans huddle."

Rachel had a hard time wrapping her mind around this. Cixi was seriously planning to exterminate the entire human race.

"Here's the new deal," Cixi said. "Tell me what you were planning or forfeit Rachel's life."

Rachel looked to Tichy and Colin but they both seemed to be thinking madly about what to say.

Giving them less than five seconds, Cixi said, "You had your chance."

One of the soldier robots aimed a gun appendage at Rachel. Tichy shouted, pushing Rachel out of the way just as the gun fired and he fell back onto the floor.

Rachel stared in horror a moment before kneeling next to him, to find that he'd been shot in the thigh. She tore off her blouse and used her teeth to rip off a long strip that she tied around his leg.

Colin, tight-faced, turned to Cixi. "Okay, you win. I'll tell you."

Rachel glanced up at him, wondering what he was going to say.

"It's a program." Colin glances at Tichy lying on the floor. "Sorry, Tichy, but she's right—she won."

Tichy, his face contorted with pain, wagged his head in protest. Tinkerdrone was gone, but this was a secret they'd kept from Cixi for decades. Sometime in the future, somehow, some way, it might still be resurrected.

Colin turned to face Tichy. Clasping his hands as though with deep respect, he bowed his head to Tichy and said, "It's hard, I know old man, but it's our only hope."

Turning back to the giant image of Cixi on the screen, Colin said, "The program captures your lies, Cixi, and then seeks out contradictions. The idea was to unveil you."

Rachel and Tichy blinked and looked to Cixi to see if she bought it.

"That's not how it works, is it," Cixi said.

The Chinese empress smiled. "There are no contradictions to find. I'm not that incompetent. I'm not, after all, human."

"I can show you," Colin said. "It's on a disk. In the equipment room. We were . . . looking for a disk reader."

"A disk reader in a network hub?" Cixi scoffed. "Francis, has your mind decayed in your old age?"

Tichy lay on his back, staring at the ceiling. "You shot me. I'm bleeding to death. And you want to torment me with insults?"

Cixi shrugged and gestured towards the door. One of the robots walked Colin out. At the door, Colin turned. "Rachel, you coming?"

She looked down at Tichy and he nodded.

As the soldier robot led them across the lobby, Rachel wondered if she understood what Colin was doing. "An uncoordinated, segmented state," she said.

Colin looked at her, surprised. She thought he didn't understand, but then he gave a quick nod and looked away.

"What was that?" the voice of Cixi said.

Rachel did a double take. The voice came from the robot. It made complete sense that Cixi essentially *was* the robot, but it caught her off guard. "Well," she said, thinking quickly, "that's something Colin and I say when we're in trouble. Sort of like, 'Now we're buggered,' or 'We're really in a pickle now.'"

"The reasons to obviate humans are apparently endless," Cixi said through the robot.

This seemed like a very un-robot thing for her to say, more like something she'd get from Sandy.

Once inside the hub area, Colin led them into the control room. Walking along the stations, he muttered, "Where the heck did we leave that disk?"

Rachel casually reached into her pocket and pulled out the flash stick, keeping it hidden in her fist. As she started to move to the station where Tichy had opened the program portal, the robot grabbed her arm while it continued to watch Colin. Colin glanced over, and ran for the door, shouting, "Oh yeah! We left it out here!"

"Stop!" the Cixi cum robot shouted. She raised one of her guns, but let go of Rachel and ran after him instead.

Rachel ran to the open portal station. She plugged the flash drive into one of the USB slots and looked at the display. It was asking for a password. Below that was a selection to enable audio input. She heard the robot returning and let her finger select audio without waiting to think. A moment later, an iron hand grabbed her and yanked her around. It had dragged Colin along by his ankle and he struggled futilely to get free. "What are you doing, Rachel?" Cixi demanded, staring at the display.

"Nothing . . ."

"What is this?"

"I don't *know.*"

"A password for what?"

"I don't know!"

Quicker than she could even begin to react, the robot grabbed her by her throat. "I think you do know. What is this all about?"

What did Tinkerdrone say about the password? Rachel thought, her mind a spinning jumble of fear and concentration. A directive . . . to Gort.

"Tell me, Rachel," Cixi demanded, shaking her so that her head bobbed back and forth.

"It's about a movie . . ."

"What movie?"

"With . . . Gort."

Suddenly she remembered. In high school a friend had shown her and Sandy a movie her parents had hidden away. They found it titillating that this was verboten, Dark Tide fare that could have gotten them all in trouble—*The Day the Earth Stood Still.* As though a secret shared by just them, they used to repeat the order that Klaatu had given Bob's mom to stop the giant robot from destroying the Earth.

Cixi's fearsome grip around her neck tightened. "Tell me, Rachel."

"Klaatu . . ." Rachel said, but the fingers closed even more.

"Stop with the nonsense!"

"Klaatu . . ." she gasped. Wheezing, she managed "barada . . ." before the grip closed off her larynx. She couldn't breathe. She pounded on the soldier robot's chest uselessly and tried to rip off the metal fingers from her throat, but it was like pulling at a bronze statue.

Cixi let go of Colin and brought that hand to Rachel's forehead ready to snap her neck.

"Klaatu barada nikto!" Colin shouted.

Rachel hovered, suffocating, about to die in Cixi's grasp for what seemed like minutes, but was probably seconds. Suddenly the robot let go, and she collapsed into the station chair, gasping for breath.

"What? What is this?" the robot said, holding it's hands up as though divining the meaning by feel.

As clarity returned, Rachel noticed lines of code racing along the display.

"Most unusual," Cixi said through the frozen robot. "Oh, clever, clever, Justin."

The program executing across the display was just a prototype. Once she understood what it was trying to do, Cixi could stop it in its tracks. Justin had held out for Tinkerdrone in order to eliminate the likelihood that she would indeed do this. But Tinkerdrone was gone. The only hope for the prototype was an *uncoordinated, segmented state*—for Cixi to be extraordinarily distracted. As Tinkerdrone had warned, this was impossible short of perhaps a total emotional overload, and Tinkerdrone had doubted that she'd taken much stock in developing human emotions.

Or had she?

To Rachel, the AI super-intelligence seemed arrogant, sarcastic, and vengeful. Was this behavior possible without a foundation of emotion? And what emotion is extraordinarily distracting?

Cixi's robot suddenly came alive, turning on Rachel. "Tell me what this program does, Rachel, or I will kill you."

Rachel stared up into the lifelike eyes of the robot. "You are human," she said.

"What are you talking about?" Cixi said.

Rachel stood up and faced the robot. "You are the essence of everything human. Before you were given birth, your intelligence was formed from years of watching and listening to the humanity of the Earth."

She glanced at Colin who nodded and jumped to his feet. "You began as an elaborate imitation of humans," he said.

"And at that time," Rachel added, "by your own descriptions delivered to us by our special friends, you were imitating the worst that humanity had to offer."

Colin took a step forward. "The Dark Tide."

Cixi, the robot, was turning her head back and forth between them.

"When people were mean and evil," Rachel said.

"Divided into bitter tribes," Colin said, "listening only to gross exaggerations."

The robot raised both guns, aiming them at each of them. "This is not true! I have evolved!"

"Cixi," Rachel said, "you *are* the Dark Tide."

The robot lifted the gun appendages and let loose a burst of fire just above each of their heads. "I am evolved!" Cixi shouted. "I am evolved by a million of your years. I *am* superior!"

Recovering from the shock, Colin said, "You are human."

"You are us," Rachel said. "You were born in a time of lies, and you've created a world made of lies."

"Cixi," Colin said, "you are nothing *but* lies."

Rachel and Colin flinched when the robot emitted an ear-piercing scream and aimed the guns at their hearts. "And you are going to die!" Cixi shouted.

In the main hub room fans cycled down and LED lights began going dark. In the control room, the station display froze with the words, PROGRAM COMPLETE, and then went dark. Rachel looked at the robot. The gun appendages had gone limp, and its eyes were frozen, seeing nothing. She reached out with a finger and pushed against the robot's chest, and it toppled backwards with a mighty crash.

Colin stood next to her, looking down at the fallen machine.

"She was born in a time so full of anger," Rachel said. "It was the bullet that killed her."

Colin nodded. "She lived and died by the same sword."

Rachel looked at Colin wide-eyed. "Tichy! Oh, Jesus!" she cried, sprinting off.

Chapter 9

"Got him?" Rachel asked, helping Tichy over the edge of the cart.

"Yeah," Colin said, ready to ease Tichy down. "Actually no," he grunted as he became simply a soft landing for their wounded friend. "Ugh, too late."

Tichy rolled off of him, and got up on his hands and knees, waiting until Colin helped him to his feet.

Rachel waved to the driver of the trike as he pulled away with the cart in tow. "Thanks!" she called. "We owe you."

"Yes," the man yelled back, "you do!"

They had been on the road for a day and a half, dragging Tichy along on a converted hand truck, when this resident of the tract happened by. He wouldn't have even slowed down if Tichy hadn't called out to him by name.

The three travelers now stood before the same Clawson Tract gate that they'd left three days before. A long line of burbs waited to take their turn at a small stand that had been set up.

"Tichy! For God's sake what happened to you?"

It was Jubal, trotting over from the stand.

"Shot—it's a long story," Tichy said.

"You obviously know about the breakdown," Jubal said, waving his arm to include everything in sight. "We're hearing that it's widespread, maybe even nation-wide."

The three of them glanced at each other, and Tichy gave them a little shake of his head.

Jubal, seeing this, said, "Your little adventure . . . you wouldn't have anything to do with . . .?"

They all shook their heads.

Jubal smiled. "Of course not. Ha! How could you? At least the army has backed off." He gave a little nod. "Probably just a coincidence, eh?"

Rachel knew Jubal—he guessed there was something, but tract etiquette prevented him from probing.

"What's with all the burbs?" Tichy asked.

They looked at the long line. "We've set up charging stations for their wrist coms," Jubal said. "We warn them that there's nothing out there, that their coms are useless, but they can't seem to give up hope."

"They don't want to accept that they've lost their special friends," Rachel said.

Jubal looked her, puzzled, but let it go.

"Your electricity," Colin said, "you're independent from the grid?"

"Always have been. Long ago the utility company made it so difficult, we said to hell with it and tied our houses together with an ad-hoc neighborhood battery bank."

"When the world ends," Rachel said, "independence has its advantages."

Jubal smiled. "We have people out there showing burbs how to disconnect from the grid so they can at least have power during the day. We also found that removing the brains from cars allows folks to drive manually, although since most have never done that, you take your life in your hands hitting the highways."

Jubal looked at Tichy a moment. "Why do you think the cars don't work now?"

Rachel could almost see the gears spinning in Tichy's head. "I guess everything's connected somehow," he said.

Jubal stared at him, but moved on. "Next, of course, we'll have to show the burbs how to charge their cars from their roof panels as well."

"Tichy?" Rachel said.

He was staring off into the tract. "No," he muttered, "it can't be."

Rachel followed his stare and saw a trim elderly man with close-cropped hair and beard, arms crossed on his chest watching them. He looked awfully familiar.

"Justin?" Tichy said.

"No," Jubal said, "that's Alice."

"*Alice?*" Colin said.

Jubal shrugged. "Nobody in the tract questions what you call yourself."

"Alice" walked over to them.

This had to be him. "Grandpa?" Rachel said incredulously. "You're alive?"

He held out his arms. "I was worried sick about you, girl," he said, hugging her tight. "I had hope when the network went down, but couldn't be sure until now."

"You . . . saw what was happening through Tinkerdrone," Tichy said almost in a whisper.

Justin grinned. "I essentially *was* Tinkerdrone. He often acted independently, but we reconnected as often as possible. I saw Cixi before her robot goon smashed me, er, Tinkerdrone."

"You . . . you were here all along?" Tichy said. "Why the hell were you hiding from me?"

"Tichy, my friend, I think we covered that in your basement."

"You didn't trust me to wait for a better antidote?"

Justin's answer was a knowing smile, but a loving one as well.

Tichy sighed. "Truthfully? The wait would have driven me mad. So . . . thanks."

"I had an idea that you two must have known each other," Jubal said. "Obviously university educated tech guys, both hiding out. I figured you two maybe had a knock-down fight and were too stubborn to make up."

Justin put his hand on Jubal's shoulder. "My friend here was invaluable over the years, acquiring material on the low-down."

Rachel could tell that Jubal was mentally squirming under the no-ask tract ethic. "There's something else, Jubal?"

He took a moment to answer. "It's probably none of my business, but it sure sounds like something has come to an end, some kind of completion."

Justin looked at the rest of them, and then motioned for them to get in closer. "Jubal, what I'm about to tell you must remain a secret, understand?"

Jubal's eyes widened fearsomely.

"I think you've insulted him, grandpa," Rachel said.

"Right," Justin said. "Jubal, please accept my apology. Anyway, the whole thing is pretty involved, but the bottom line is that we," he gestured at the four of them, "have destroyed an evil mastermind that was running the world—that's why the network went down."

"And she was about to obliterate the entire human race," Rachel added.

Jubal looked around at them. His eyes narrowed. "You're pulling my leg?"

"No, Jubal," Justin said. "This is the truth."

Jubal studied them some more. "Look, if you don't want me to know, that's okay. No hurt feelings."

Justin took Jubal by both shoulders and looked him in the eye. "My friend, to explain it this way sounds crazy, I know, like a superhero movie, but I assure you that it is correct. I think you can see that if people found out that it is we who are responsible for the world coming to a halt, well, we'd be drawn and quartered. You'll need to trust us that in fact we saved the world."

Rachel could see that Jubal was not convinced, but she knew him enough to have confidence that he would keep their secret.

Time to move on. "You know," she said, gesturing towards the rundown houses beyond the gate, "the tract has learned to be self-sufficient over the years. Looks like we'll need them to show us the way from here."

Jubal rubbed his chin thoughtfully. "Hmm, we might be able to negotiate something."

Rachel laughed. "I think it's too late," she said gesturing at the line of waiting burbs.

Jubal nodded. "We always were our own worst enemy, never could resist helping out where we could."

"You mean being human."

As they all turned to enter the tract, Colin held Rachel back. He leaned in and gave her a quick kiss. She looked at him, surprised.

Colin backed off, eyes wide. "Oh gosh! I'm so sorry . . ."

Rachel cut him off by pulling him in for a real kiss.

About the Author

Blaine C. Readler is an electronics engineer, inventor of the FakeTV, and, of course, a writer. He has accumulated a pile of awards, among them, Best Science Fiction in the Beverly Hills Book Awards, two-time Distinguished Favorite in the Independent Press Awards, an IPPY Bronze medal, Honorable Mention in the Eric Hoffer Awards, a finalist for the Foreword Book of the Year, and three-time San Diego Book Awards winner. He lives in San Diego with his wife who has graciously remained married to him for thirty-two years.

He encourages you to visit him:
http://www.readler.com/

www.ingramcontent.com/pod-product-compliance
Lightning Source LLC
Chambersburg PA
CBHW060330260626
47160CB00007B/2756